Praise for FLORIDA

"Beautiful and mean and elegantly wry, this story of an abandoned girl . . . is also the story of storytelling—and how it develops as a means to order one's disordered world."

—*The Believer*

"It is astonishing to encounter a book like *Florida*, which reads like something new entirely . . . Each individual fragment is a prose poem, complete as an artifact, an object of beauty. The fragments also represent a bold attempt to represent memory as it is experienced . . . Schutt's remarkable facility with language renders this approach, which is rightfully experimental, in a flowing voice given to clarity, accessibility."

—*The Antioch Review*

"A dazzling start for a writer we want to hear from again."

—*Kirkus Reviews*

"Schutt's perceptive handling of time capsules embedded in Alice's memory . . . marks her as a writer to watch."

—*Booklist*

"Christine Schutt's sad and funny novel of a little girl adrift amid a group of childish adults has the same brilliancy of close observation that distinguished her collection of stories *Nightwork*. Everything the child sees is unstable, but the fixed intensity of her gaze grounds her chaotic home life and almost confers a logic on it. *Florida* is an amazing achievement."

—John Ashbery, author of *Where Shall I Wander*

"Writing with razor-sharp observation, in *Florida* Christine Schutt has created an admirably precise, spare, and yet detailed portrait of the contingencies that give rise to a young girl's anguish and her stubborn endurance against all odds."

—Lydia Davis, author of *Samuel Johnson Is Indignant*

"*Florida* is a haunting work, part narrative, part dream; its images are gripping, its situation compelling. The writing is unforgettable. A wholly original endeavor."

—Mary Gordon, author of *Spending*

"This is a portrait of bravery and this is a portrait of an artist. When Schutt grinds her pen against the ground, we expect it to bleed."

—Diane Williams, author of *Romancer Erector*

"A young child's father dies mysteriously, her mother is by and by sent away to 'the San': in the midst of an upper-class American hell, more ice than fire, the child's hard-found days and nights break into language—into poetry, really—which saves, and becomes, a life. I am awed by this book's wealth, intensity, and painful beauty."

—Jean Valentine, author of *The Cradle of the Real Life*

"Mastery of prose, according to Isaac Babel, is achieved not when no word can be added but when no word can be taken away. That is the kind of mastery the author of *Florida* has achieved. As for the story, it is simply about the most important things: childhood, family, love, identity, storytelling itself, and the saving power of memory and imagination."

—Sigrid Nunez, author of *For Rouenna*

"Christine Schutt's *Florida* offers us a searing vision of the emotional and material currency of a family's life. This brave, beautiful, wry book is about loss, yes, but also about the obdurate wisdom that grows in the places where the heart is broken."

—Dawn Raffel, author of *Carrying the Body*

FLORIDA

FLORIDA

CHRISTINE SCHUTT

A Harvest Book • Harcourt, Inc.

Orlando   Austin   New York   San Diego   Toronto   London

www.HarcourtBooks.com

First published by TriQuarterly Books in 2004

Excerpt from "The Summer Anniversaries" appeared in Donald Justice,
The Summer Anniversaries (Middleton, Conn.: Wesleyan University
Press, 1960), and is reprinted by permission of the publisher.

Library of Congress Cataloging-in-Publication Data
Schutt, Christine, 1948–
Florida / Christine Schutt.—1st Harvest ed.
p. cm.
1. Maternal deprivation—Fiction. 2. Young women—Fiction.
3. Orphans—Fiction. I. Title.
PS3569.C55555F56 2005
813.54—dc22   2005046354
ISBN-13: 978-0-15-603054-0   ISBN-10: 0-15-603054-3

Text set in Sabon

Printed in the United States of America
First Harvest edition 2005
A C E G I J H F D B

TO SALLY ANN AND TO CHESTER

FLORIDA

MOTHER

She was on her knees and rubbing her back against parts of the house and backing into corners and sliding out from under curtains, rump polishing the floor, and she was saying, "Sit with me, Alice." She was saying, "Talk to me. Be a daughter. Tell me what you've been doing." She spoke uninflectedly, as if thinking of something else—the dishes to do, drawers to line, clotted screens to clean out with a toothpick. Handles missing, silver gone, and a Walter in the next room unwilling to leave!

Bitch, bitch, bitch, the sound the broomsticks made against the floor in Mother's nettled cleaning and talking to herself, asking, "What am I doing? What does it look like I am doing?"

"You are stupid," I overheard Walter say to my mother. "You'd be better off dead."

And Walter was as smart as any professor; he was the first to admit it, saying to my mother, "Why are you so stupid?" Stupid about composers and who was playing. Stupid about motherhood and about how much money she had. Why didn't she know, why didn't she plan ahead? Why was it always up to him to think it out for her? Walter sat in the armchair and sipped at his whiskey and held out a hand no one took.

All day he sipped warm whiskey from a highball glass. He

smoked cigarettes; he listened to his records on Mother's stereo—crashing, oppressive, classical sound. If Walter spoke, it was to shout for it, "Louder!" when I was thinking the music was already too loud. Enough, I was thinking, creeping nearer to the stereo myself with other ideas for music. The composer's portrait on the long-playing album cover looked, I thought, like Walter. They shared a melancholy nose and disappointed mouth, old-fashioned eyeglasses, Einstein hair.

I never saw him in the sun or on a sidewalk, never at the porch or beside the car about to open a door for Mother. I never saw Walter laughing. The brown yolks of his eyes had broken and smeared to a dog-wild and wounded gaze. He was not handsome; yet I looked long at the length of him slant in a chair with his drink.

No man Mother knows seems to work. They go away sometimes in the day and come back wrinkled. They come back to us and sit half the night half concealed by the wing chair's wings. They drink and listen to music.

"The Germans," Walter said. "Schubert."

Sometimes I found Walter crying in the chair, and once I found him in the morning on the downstairs couch in a twisted sheet with Mother.

With my father it had been different.

At the restaurant one winter afternoon, months before he died, we made a scene; we dragged the waiter into our story; we were the last to leave. I danced around the heavy black tables and the matching chairs; I spun on the barstools and watched the TV. Mother cried, and she let herself be kissed.

"We're drunk," Mother said. "We are."

"Open wide," my father was saying to her and then to me, "open wider."

One winter afternoon—an entire winter—it was my father who was taking us. Father and Mother and I, we were going to Florida—who knew for how long? I listened in at the breakfast table whenever I heard talk of sunshine. I asked questions about our living there that made them smile. We all smiled a lot at the breakfast table. We ate sectioned fruit capped with bleedy maraschinos—my favorite! The squeezed juice of the grapefruit was grainy with sugar and pulpy, sweet, pink. "Could I have more?" I asked, and my father said sure. In Florida, he said it was good health all the time. No winter coats in Florida, no boots, no chains, no salt, no plows and shovels. In the balmy state of Florida, fruit fell in the meanest yard. Sweets, nuts, saltwater taffies in seashell colors. In the Florida we were headed for the afternoon was swizzled drinks and cherries to eat, stem and all: "Here's to you, here's to me, here's to our new home!" One winter afternoon in our favorite restaurant, there was Florida in our future while I was licking at the foam on the fluted glass, biting the rind and licking sugar, waiting for what was promised: the maraschino cherry, ever-sweet every time.

MOTHER

A different winter and a different kind of winter, the air peated with dark and me swimming through it, I saw, or thought I saw, the car's red lights receding: *good-bye, good-bye.* By then Mother's nose had been broken, so that whenever she spoke, she sounded stuffed up. "Good-bye, good-riddance," she was saying to Walter when we were caught up in our Florida.

Mother promised that in our Florida, hers and mine, we would get a bird, a large, showy bird, a talker, someone who could say more than "hiya" and his name, but a sleek and brightly beaked bird—a talker, excited, scrabbling on the bar, saying, "Alice, Alice"—a bird that would live on and on, not some dumb Polly.

Mother promised that in Florida I could hold the hand mirror to the sun to start a fire; in Florida there would be no need of matches. "The heat," she said, "the steamy heat, the pink sand. Try to imagine."

Mother's toenails winked in the foil bed we knew for Florida. Her toenails were polished in a black-red put on thick. Her fingernails she wore as they were: skin-colored, square-cut, clear. The ragged moons on some nails she showed me signaled deprivations—not enough milk or an unrelieved fever—such losses, experienced in a mother's womb, could be read on the teeth, Mother told me, when the teeth were discolored. She said, "Look at Walter." Mother's terrible Walter had grown up in a place always warm and yet his smile, Mother said, revealed his sorrows.

He covered up his teeth when he was smiling; he hid behind his hands. Caught chewing, he looked caught. He looked angry or dismayed. Walter frowned at me a lot, or that was how it seemed to me when Mother wasn't home. With this Walter there were no foam drinks, no maraschino cherries, no promises and kisses. He brooded, he swore, he drank.

The day Walter left, the phone was ringing and the TV was never shut off. Lights came on. There was crying. Car doors slammed, cars started, high beams swept the drive. We might have been a TV show was how it looked to me from the window where I saw a woman in a nightgown prepared to stop the car by merely standing in front of it. Mother held out her arms and was, I thought, pleading please to stay or to take her, too, but please, not on any account, please not to leave. "No, no, no, no, no," she was crying. "Please!"

Then Walter was yelling from the car at me, saying, "Your mother's the one. She's a crazy, bloody woman! She wants all of my money!"

"Get out!" I shouted, and then Mother shouted, too, "Get out, get out! Leave us alone!"

Wavy grounds, old trees, floating nurses. Mother called it "the San." I visited only once—too scared to go again—and remember that Mother's shirtwaist dress no longer fit and strained the pin that pinned her. "Ouchie," she said, a baby-voiced girl, and she fiddled off the pinhead then started to cry, saying, "Now I can't stand up!" speaking as if to someone else though there was no one else but me in her room at the time. "I can't see my little girl off. My skirt will fall down and my Alice will be embarrassed." I was embarrassed by her and glad to leave Mother behind and took the stairs, which were faster, to the car where Aunt Frances was talking to a doctor, and Arthur was waiting to drive us away.

Arthur had, as part of his job, driving to do. Arthur did the errand-driving in any-old-day clothes, but he dressed in a coat when he drove Aunt Frances anywhere. With me he wore his leather jacket—smelly, cracked, collared in a matted yarn, brown. I don't remember what he was wearing that day when he drove Mother to the San. It was cold, I remember.

"Miss Alice," Arthur had called to Mother, "please get in."

Mother was wearing the falling-leaves coat in the falling-leaf colors, a thing blown it was she seemed, past its season, a brittle skittering across the icy snow to where Arthur stood by the car, fogged in.

✛ ✛ ✛

I attended to the drama of Mother's clothes, the smoke-thin nightgown she wore before Arthur came; I wanted it. She wisped through the house in this nightgown and eschewed electric light and carried candles. "Go to sleep," she had said, come upon me spying, and I said to her, "You, too!" but Mother was awake and moving through the house and out across the snow—Mother shouting back at me, "You're not invited!" Later she cried, and I sat under the crooked roof of her arm and felt her gagged and heaving sorrow. "If your father were here . . ."

But my father was dead and my name was hers and everyone said I was surely her daughter, so why did she leave me except that she did? The next day she was off to her Florida, and I was off to mine.

The coiled trail of the car lighter in the dark reminded me of
Mother when Uncle Billy was smoking and supervising Arthur
as he carried to the backdoor and into the kitchen roped boxes
from Mother's house. Suitcases, clocks, chiming clocks, more
boxes. Uncle Billy held out the fur hat to me. "Where she is
now," he said, "your mother won't need it." The hat in my
hand came alive; I felt it warm and breathing and felt the weak
heat hushing from the baseboards against my ankles, my feet.

Arthur was driving again. He was driving past shapes crouched
in sleeping fields, past unplowed snows and smokeless chim-
neys. Grimaced light and hard snow, loose doors, abandon-
ment. "Is it time to go to Uncle Billy's?" I asked. "Are we here
already?" Here at Arlette's, at Nonna's, at Uncle Billy's, at
Nonna's, no logic to the rotation, no meaning I could figure
except to know the first house and the last at different ends of
the lake. Uncle Billy's house was first—brick walk, cold wind,
water, water roughing against the shore. I saw the water's darkness in the distance when so much else was under snow. But
the ledges from the rock gardens jutted out like tongues; and
the trees, standing before the moon, were reprimanded. The
moon was a scold.

"Outside after dark is for animals," Aunt Frances said.
"Come inside where it is warm."

Hardly warm! The old sashes rattled in the windows—

hundreds, all sides—so that a cold air rimmed the rooms and rooms and rooms of Uncle Billy's house. "There!" someone pointed: Great-Granddaddy in an accomplished pose, painted a year shy of his dying. I looked at his eyes, and it seemed to me he did not want to live and that Mother was right: Great-Granddaddy had rushed into his dying.

Uncle Billy said to Aunt Frances, "That sounds like something my sister would say," and Aunt Frances said to me, "I don't know what your mother allowed, but here we talk only of living," and she took away my picture books of pyramids of rings and shoes. "Depressing photographs," she said, and she gave me books on animals instead. I liked these, too, and I liked the new haircut; it was better than what Mother usually did. Mother who would never fix me. "I can't do French braids," Mother had once confessed. "Look at me! Wear a hat!"

Aunt Frances, holding up clothes from my suitcase—socks, shirt, the same hat—said, "Why aren't these name tagged?" And she gave my clothes to Arlette. Dragged hems, belts broken, Arlette could fix almost anything provided I helped.

"Hold still!" Arlette said, or "we'll go to Miss Pearl. Hold still!" Little wiggler, little bungler, always dirtying herself! "I remember," Arlette said, and then she told such stories I had just as soon forget.

On any day in the week, I wanted to be away from Uncle Billy's and in the car with Arthur driving past where I once lived. Down Lawn and across School was how I had walked for all of my life; I had walked to where a far-below, mean-looking river dropped at my feet: Main Street, the original. Walked north, away from water and local business, Main

Street was houses: Sloane's and Doctor Humber's and Miss Pearl's—old, old Miss Pearl's, with her pointy tongue for sewing, who crawled below my skirts and never pricked me. Her porch windows snapped in the cold; I heard them despite passing fast, and I ducked, not wanting to be seen in Uncle Billy's gem-like car. I did not want my old block to see me. I was avoiding the scalded daughter with the patched-over face. Friends once, and friendless, we had walked far apart through the fields behind our houses on the small side streets.

"My street!" I called after, going Arthur's way to school, airport, Arlette's—wherever it was he was taking me.

"Pull over there," I sometimes said rudely. "Park there and wait, Arthur. No one will see me. I just want to look."

My old house, the original.

The window I looked through showed open doors and light from windows unseen, and I wondered what the rooms were like upstairs. Had the upstairs been emptied, too, and would I never again see our house?

Uncle Billy was going to the desert—again! We were all going to the desert, all except Arthur. And Arlette, too, was staying behind. Arlette was minding the lake house, the one Aunt Frances loved best. Aunt Frances did not like the desert. "I'm a snow bird," she said; nevertheless, Aunt Frances packed. She ordered sleeveless shirts for me with my initials on the collars. Sleeveless shirts in March—imagine! We were shucking off our winter coats; we were traveling light: "Good-bye, Arthur, (good-riddance, Arlette), good-bye."

The desert was a vacation Uncle Billy paid for—no bargains, no deals—but here Uncle Billy hoped to make money, *more* money, unusually, of course, in the desert.

In the desert Uncle Billy carried a gun. The desert birds were a spring green or dirt color, I remember this, and Uncle Billy's gun and the mountains and the trek we took after the Dutchman's lost mine. I was ten—ten was my age when Mother left for good, and this sleep-over life began. I was sleeping at my Uncle Billy's desert house that time we took the Dutchman's trek, and I drank my water early, and Uncle Billy would not share his. He said, "Let that be a lesson to you, sweetie."

I swam and swam in Uncle Billy's pool.

I wrote to Arthur. I asked about the snow. I told him maybe I wouldn't come back. Spring after spring, I wrote this same message: *I love it here. Maybe I won't come back.*

✛ ✛ ✛

But Arthur was waiting in the car for me.

Arthur was waiting, was paid to be waiting to drive me from house to house, to Uncle Billy's winter house and then to Arlette's shack, to Nonna's, Uncle Billy's again, Nonna's, Uncle Billy's—Arthur was stoutly, conspicuously waiting for me, and I was embarrassed to be seen with him. Standing outside of the car, simply taking up my luggage, Arthur looked uglier than when even Mother left. His teeth, his nose. "Hello," I said with a brushed-past hug. "Arthur," I said, insisting on his name. I was ashamed of my cool behavior, yet I didn't want anyone to see Arthur and to think he was my father. My father was handsome!

Arthur was waiting in the car for me; in front of school or after lessons, Arthur was waiting in Uncle Billy's formal car, a blue-black, deep green, the same color as the stone Aunt Frances wore on her wedding-ring finger, a color stippled in the light, expensive.

Arthur called the car the Emerald Gem, and he washed the car weekly and dried it with a chamois. I helped.

I ran the chamois through the wringer and picked out gravel in the bristles of the brush.

Not much talking between us unless I asked, and I didn't ask but came to conclusions from the way things looked. The way things looked made me think Arthur was sad, and I was sad for him. No immediate family, no friends, poor Arthur in overalls, smelling of oil and earth. His lace-up shoes had a bulbous toe, and the empty crown of his baseball cap stuck up stupidly. He swooped off the cap, saying, "Yes, Mister, Yes, Miss, Yes, Miss Frances" to the orders from the boss, to Uncle Billy or his wife. Arthur's hair was sweated flat, his forehead grooved. Poor Arthur, left to do what I couldn't do, he looked tired.

"Can't I help?" I asked.

"No, stay where you are. You're help just watching."

"Can I come along then?"

"Okay," Arthur said, and Uncle Billy said, too, but more often, "No, Alice, you stay here. . . ." And if I didn't ride quietly, didn't obey, what happened then? Banished to the backseat, obliged to sit and watch as they loaded Mother's house on the U-Haul: her bed, a chest of drawers, six dining chairs, stacked. Arthur and his helpers were doing the work; Uncle Billy only bossed.

Shame, I felt, confusion, wonder, ease, the impression of a fire, a reddening light pulsed the shelter of leaves that branched across the road to Uncle Billy's house. Arthur drove. Arthur was almost always driving or waiting and waiting, often for Uncle Billy, and with only a knife to pare his nails.

"Aren't you bored?" I asked, yet another day, waiting in the Emerald Gem with Arthur and shivering despite the heat it hoarded. "Aren't you bored? Because I am." Hips passed and hems and scarf fringe and gloves, and I couldn't see past the doors to the building, the one my Uncle Billy was in, the building with the doors revolving: not him, not him.

A Monday afternoon, a Thursday afternoon—any afternoon—it might be. Uncle Billy liked surprises and he liked to surprise, and he could! "An adventure!" he said, off to find gold or sausage or slot machines (really!) whatever he could find. Every day was his own, and Uncle Billy could be late.

"You must be patient," Arthur said, which was fine, I thought, for a man dressed to wait in another man's car, but I didn't want to sit here without music. I didn't want to wait with Arthur, and I was rude. I said, "Wait for me, too," and I took off down the block on my own somewhere. Five minutes, ten, I wasn't very long away—but still. . . .

"Has Alice been good?" Uncle Billy asked, returned and turned around to look at me while Arthur drove the three of us to someplace special where Uncle Billy flashed a card at a carpeted booth that let us in for free—for free the festooned aisles of giveaways and samples, tubs, birdbaths, rug shampoos, a new and faster way to cut up food. Big girls packed in dirndls held out dips and toothpicked weenies. Raffles, contests, questionnaires, there were baskets of possibilities only waiting to be signed, and Uncle Billy was smiling broadly. "A year's worth of anything was something," he was saying, but what would he have to buy?

"The chance to go to Orlando," was what the nearest clipboard said, and Uncle Billy bought it. He was rich!

He bought Mexico City, too, and raffles for instant-retirement cash, a bird, a goat, a car called Windlass. A trip with my mother's rich brother was never entirely boring. Brochures, calling cards, glo-pink logos, Uncle Billy bought guesses and drawings, and carelessly fetched for me whatever was free— for a pet I didn't have or an ailment; but the cure spilled in the trunk and there were rolling pellets. "No more adventures, I think," Arthur was saying to me, sponging off the dashboard and the armrests. "No more or we're going to get in trouble with Aunt Frances. . . ."

The wet wind of Arthur's seriousness, that could make me

shiver; and Aunt Frances . . . and Arlette, too. They spoke in unison to me: "We know what you've been doing." Then they put up what treasures I had from my mother's, put up too high for me to reach. "Just ask," Aunt Frances said. "You won't even remember what's here, I bet." But I remembered, and I recognized Mother's plates and glasses, the felt bags of silver Mother wrote to me about, "Don't sell the silver. We can afford it."

Mother wrote me at the beginning. "This is where I am," and x'd on a card she had drawn was a beachfront high-rise, palm trees dashed in front of it.

Flowers in the folds of letters, "Smell these!"

Locks of new blond hair, "Wish you could see!"

I scorned what seemed flimsy for the cold we knew, what scant clothes Mother sent me. "Love, love, love, love," Uncle Billy read, and he held out the package with its friable contents, its hankies of printed cloth.

"I'm not wearing this," I said. "Whatever made her think I would?"

I was a prude then; I was easily embarrassed by my body and by my mother's body and how she had exposed it—remember? When the yard was under snow? Mother, sunbathing on a bed of foil Arthur had built for her, a sun-box, Arthur's homemade Florida, and Mother on her knees, waving to me—waving to the neighborhood!—her legs glossy and oiled and white, the sun invisibled in murk. "Look where I am!" Florida, Florida, no matter that we lived in the land-of-lakes state where spring was slow to come.

Arthur said to me, "No one could be happy the way she was." He said, "No one in the family was as generous . . . remember that," but I forgot.

ARTHUR

Sometimes waiting in the car with Arthur, I was a loving child—or my idea of loving—and I told him that I wanted to stay at his house, not Uncle Billy's, but Arthur's house, above Uncle Billy's garage. I wanted to stay for early supper when late light shot through water glasses to show up rims of dust we put our lips to. Disuse and absence, I saw it scumming unwashed jars full of greasy house-parts, and I felt sorry for Arthur when I visited him, and I believed that, left to stay over, I could make his evening easier, happier, less dingy—a child's conceit.

Arthur's house, although small, was oddly just as cold as Uncle Billy's—even colder, I think—four rooms he warmed with the stove set to high and left open. The space heater he carried everywhere to plug near his feet. His feet!—those shapeless stockinged bags of stones, somehow Arthur walked on them.

"Is it time to go already?" I was anxiously asking because I did and I didn't want to leave. No one was there to think he was my father, so I could love him as I might a father. I wanted Arthur to feel loved. I asked, "Is it time already? I want to stay."

This much was true: I often wanted to visit Arthur, but Uncle Billy said no; and only sometimes, as when Uncle Billy and his wife were gone, could I spend afternoons with Arthur. (The nights were that nosy Arlette's.) Then Arthur and I could forget Uncle Billy's car—that jewel, that gem—and drive the truck around Uncle Billy's estate or slosh the thaws in clattery galoshes: "Cold?" Arthur asking, and me saying, "Yes," but walking on.

My hands were red and wet and cold that time we broke through dish-thin ice in our walk along the cornfield. Arthur was wearing his ear-flapped cap, of course, and a leathery coat with a quilted lining bright enough to see by when he asked, "Do you want me to give you a ride?" It was his tired body that he was offering, yet I took it. I rode him out beyond the breakage, beyond the tangle of flagged stalks and splintered ice. The sky lifted, turned black, grew stars. At his door, slipped off in the shape that I had been, I lifted my arms to him and said, "Again?"

I could be thoughtless.

MOTHER

Once in a snow drift packed by plows come down my street, I made a snow car and sat in it for hours. Then I never went to school, or if I did, I forgot where I went and what I did there. My mother was my school and my distraction—the way she answered the door or did not answer the door but sat with just her legs crossed over the arms of the chair, and whatever she was wearing and the color or lack of color she had on her mouth and the voice she was using, such things changed every day, and I was met by someone new, sometimes with new company so instantly adoring. "Do you know how lucky you are to have such a mother?" they all of them said, and I knew what Mother had been doing—giving away again, performing. In an afternoon the boxes piled by the door with Mother saying, "And this, too, really," then helping put on, talking as she did so, buttoning the new friend, "Yes, yes," saying, "yes, this is you. You must take it," giving away my father's clothes and her clothes and my clothes—some favorites that still fit.

Mother's hands were uncared for, carelessly used. She had tried to get through winter with one glove.

Arthur said, "When she was unhappy . . . ," but I knew, I knew, I knew what she did. My mother broke her body against the weather and overused the Florida Arthur had made, the foil-lined box where she lay winter-sunning herself sick.

✢ ✢ ✢

Mother wasn't always in her Florida box. One spring she strad-
dled a chaise on the sunporch off her bedroom decorating
straw bags with miniature fruits and flowers. Picnic-lidded,
ordinary bags she turned into stories with dollhouse trinkets.
Marion Van Hueval, Goldie Fleiss, Barbara Trapp, the Willis
sisters, Mr. Horner for his wife, and all the girls in the Chester
family ordered one of Mother's bags. "Your *nonna* says it's
cheap to sell what I am doing."

My mother, I thought, was an artist and could stack whatever was at hand to make a fluffed diversion. Once Mother
emptied the pantry of fruits about to spoil and twisted them
in greenery to decorate the Christmas mantle. Another year
was a pink-flocked fir dressed in silver; the next, unflocked,
done up in tartans and candy. Uncle Billy, Aunt Frances,
Nonna, and her ancient cousins—whoever it was at whatever
holiday party—waited to see what my mother would bring
because always, *always,* she surprised them.

"Oh, Alice!" they said, protesting her extravagance but
pleased to wear what she had bought them.

At the end, just before Mother and I were parted, the game
was to follow her up the stairs when she was moving very fast
and dragging behind her the falling-leaves coat in falling-leaf
colors. Mother was dragging the coat up the stairs and saying,
"Hurry. Before Arthur gets here, we can hide." The attic, the
wood bin, her foil-lined Florida, places occurred to me. Hide,
then, but where and why from Arthur who expected us? I didn't
want to leave my mother, but I knew I had to leave her.

Mother had said into the phone, "I understand. We're packed." Mother had spoken to Uncle Billy although it was Arthur who came, who knocked on the door, who rang and called in, "Miss Alice?" We were at the foot of Mother's unmade bed and listening to Arthur calling Mother gently, "Miss Alice? Miss Alice, the car's outside warm."

From the start I believed what Uncle Billy always told me, "Your mother only needs a rest." But what home would there be for her to come home to, I wondered, and I kicked at the FOR SALE sign in the snow.

First I went to Uncle Billy's house on the frozen lake, then the desert, Uncle Billy's on the frozen lake again, in-between at Arlette's, Arthur's some afternoons, then Nonna's for a long time.

"I get thirsty," I explained to Aunt Frances, to Arlette, to Uncle Billy that time in the desert. "I won't spill."

But I spilled things that stained. I made a mess, a small disaster. I caused more than one woman to cry, "How could you! How could you when I asked you not to?"

Most often I was showing off, like that time I took the boy's tire to ride in on the river when Arlette had said, "No riding in tires! I don't care how good you can swim!" Arlette had warned me when suddenly I was spinning down the river. The tire valve was sharp against my back, but I didn't care except to sit up higher, so that I could wave from the tire and not be seen as I felt I must be seen: a girl no one knew, a visitor falling through the hole of the tire—stupid, stupid! I was saved, of course; I did not become what I had hoped I might become.

No streamy thing carried forward over cataracts, no mystery. I stayed a shapeless, wicked girl, clumsy, shy, easily embarrassed. I lived on and on, and I sometimes heard Arlette's story of the day I nearly drowned.

Blah, blah, blah, Arlette was such a big talker.

May I? Do you mind? Do you mind if I? Could I? I was asking for something of everyone all the time.

I once spent an afternoon and an evening with a veiled crone—my father's mother?—who lived on a pond in a bog of green sound: croaking frogs and crickets and brittle insects that broke like twigs. The doves made the most familiar music, and I was pacified to hear it and to see the birds so stilly perched. Yet they were common birds. The doves cooed unregarded, I thought, so I paid close attention to the doves; I made a point of looking at them. I believed then that any gesture I made was felt; I believed I could make the unhappy happy just by my attentions.

"I think you're pretty," I said with my fist around the money of a compliment, but the veiled crone asked, "Who taught you to lie like that?"

MOTHER

In a photograph I still can't find, I am wearing Mother's pin-wheel dress, so called because it twirled, and I am in mid-twirl in this dress and oversized sunglasses and high, high heels. My mouth is closed to hide my braces. I sent a copy of the picture, the only one I liked of me, to Mother. Later I sent others, but none as good; yet Mother didn't even like the pinwheel picture. She wrote, *Your face looks like a pail of worms.* Nevertheless, I went on wearing Mother's clothes: the *carumba!* skirt and the Saint-Joan velvet, the bird hat, the Colbert glasses, all the quirky accessories, the dresses with names. Handmade one-of-a-kind was what Mother had left, unusual clothes worn unusual ways: sweaters inside-out and no adornment but a mouth.

More and more that was how Mother had worn her face—all mouth.

And I was all mouth—a big mouth, fat teeth, braces. A gabber, a blabber, a gossip. At ten, eleven, twelve, even older, I wanted everyone to know my story—to know it sharply, as one who rings the wounded might, with me, at the center, reciting: My father is dead, and I am only waiting for my mother to be well enough to take me away from these houses chapped by winter. Cold in Uncle Billy's house, and I was rarely left to wander. "Read," Aunt Frances said, or "Practice the piano, but softly." I could scrutinize Uncle Billy's collections, the glass cases of sprung-winged bugs, displays of shells, black and blue stones from isolate beaches—from Mother's beach, perhaps, or wherever it was she was. The picture-postcards she sent were of bullfights, clock towers, sprigs of orange blossom. Mother was writing to me as I would to Arthur, remarking on the splendid weather, asking, "Don't you have a decent picture of yourself?"

MOTHER

~

Mother kept the photo albums and gave Arthur the stereo. The silver was for me though there were pieces missing— asparagus tongs, toast holders, candlesnuffs, and coasters. The paintings, well, the paintings, the paintings she didn't know. She hadn't decided.

"I'm going to want them someday," was what she had said.

In the end Mother left behind a lot of clothes; and Aunt Frances donated the best of them to school. The famous bird hat, several wigs, the shoes some Rick had bought her— fantastical—I saw them again in school plays. I saw the hat, and a boy I had a crush on wore the hair. Aunt Frances had said, "Your mother won't see many parties where she is," and Uncle Billy had agreed. Aunt Frances and Uncle Billy had always spoken in agreement on Mother. Sunday phone calls, for instance. Remember? "Are they doing you any good?" Aunt Frances asking, and Uncle Billy asking, too. "Do you think it's helpful your mother hears you cry?"

"No," was how I answered.

"Then why?"

I shrugged. I couldn't always believe myself how much I missed my mother, but I did. It was tiring to be a guest, yet I was fearful to admit how I felt and kept saying, *thank you*, instead. I wanted to be agreeable. I wanted new clothes and I was often happy and happily dressed in cochina slippers and ruffled skirts. So what was there to cry about really—*really*? I listened to the way Aunt Frances said, "How quiet it is now!" and I knew what she meant, how the day had purpose. The pot was on the boil and beading the hood of the stove; the smell was of food just now soft. Here was comfort: Aunt Frances's kitchen. Here no food went bad but was fed to those masked scavengers, those silly raccoons. Uncle Billy put out scraps, and at his June party a bowl of champagne.

"What for?" Aunt Frances asked.

"Oh, just to see what might happen."

On the night of Uncle Billy's June party, the summer I was twelve and went away to camp, Uncle Billy said Mother might come home and might just want me back. What did I think about that?

I thought about how Mother would arrive—driving too fast and slamming the car door in a dust though the driveway was paved.

I thought about the speed of life with Mother and how, despite the uncertainty, the noise, the mess, the shame, her company was as big as the movies, and I missed her.

I was afraid, too. Here was often hard, but did I want wherever home would be with Mother?

The air then was coppery with music and from as far away as the far field where Arthur was parking cars, I could hear Uncle Billy's June party.

Oh, let's just steal this car and drive on! is what I wanted to say to Arthur.

Sometimes the dream was: I steal the car with Mother. She is well, steady, the kind of woman she can be—has been, was on occasion—the kind who says, "This is how we get there";

and she gets us there; and we have not been long on the road. The mother, who is the mother I account my favorite person, has packed enough to drink so no one goes thirsty. In some dreams there is a lap robe—cashmere, which made sense—cashmere: It was all my mother wore in sweaters, also cashmere mittens, tams, scarves. "Hand it over now, dear, I'm freezing. But you like it?" Mother asked. "So wear it. You can have it. It looks better on you." Such exchange as this was real; I didn't dream it; I had heard it from Mother a lot of the time. Mother could be lavish, yet I told Arthur that she was not—no, never really had been giving.

"She was always thankful to me. Thankful for a nail. *Thank you, thank you, thank you, Arthur.* She cried over the suntan box I made her."

Florida, where was it, I wondered, but nobody knew.

Some of Mother's clothes I had seen. The staircase skirt, for instance, floor-length and swishy, the staircase skirt was used in lots of school plays with difficult women in them given to long, hurtful speeches. These women had trembling sensibilities; these women gripped handkerchiefs and vials and knives. They were dangerous and vacant. Their exorbitance drove the play. *I know that woman* was what I said when I first saw such a woman.

In life Mother had wept to leave me and she raised a bandaged arm to wave good-bye.

"Your momma had one of them wiener dogs," Arlette said, "black, slick as a bean, yappy and scaredy—a little mean. His name was Bobbie, but your *nonna* called him Boobly—he was that stupid, still your daddy had bought him—so. So one day your momma forgets to close that fence Arthur put around the house, and Boobly takes off and into the neighbor's yard and kills a momma cat and all her little kitties. That dog! He used to eat his own poo and you'd kiss him!"

MOTHER

~ ⌣ ~

"Can I stay with you?" was what I asked Arthur when I got to
Uncle Billy's house, and Arthur said no.

Arthur said, "It's Uncle Billy's."

And the next night and the next night until I lost count of
the nights I spent there in the house full of complete collections, sets and settings, hammered silver Christmas spoons
and Dedham plates and books: a no-touch house. "Only
look," Aunt Frances said, and I looked.

"The dust!" Arlette cried, and my Aunt Frances cried, too,
both of them with rags they slapped at books, yet Uncle Billy
brought home more—more books, more figurines with china
collars made to look like lace and sharp to touch.

"Don't!" the women warned, unwrapping plates smeary
with newsprint and cold from sitting in the trunk. Rhine
wines, cordials, flute champagnes. Arthur was carrying in
more boxes; they popped when slit open and exhaled. The
women were unwrapping Mother's house. That is what I saw
on the table, plates I had eaten from. I knew the knife marks,
the slashes made by Mother with her arms around my neck
and cutting up my food from behind.

"More?" someone was asking in an astonished voice—more
of just about anything anyone could think of: shoes, salt-shakers,
candlesnuffs.

Uncle Billy was promising more if I promised to be good, more souvenirs from wherever he was going if the requests he made were met. The requests he made were not too many: Use Kleenex, don't snuffle; stop picking at your thumbs. *Until I am back* or *while I am away* was how Uncle Billy started. "I want you to be good." His wife and Arlette and Arthur—all the help—heard him say, "I want you to be good, Alice. Do you hear me? Alice?"

I didn't.

As soon as Uncle Billy was gone, Aunt Frances caught me at the cupboards, fitting my thumb in Mother's thumb-cut crystal glasses. "Snooping!" she said. "Your mother liked to snoop, too. Did you know that? Next time, ask."

I was twelve when I swore I would never be like Mother although privately I still missed her very much. Once, I asked Arthur to drive me again to where she was, drive me in the jewel, my Uncle Billy's car, that was emerald at night and took the light richly. Under the streetlights we were driving, under the downtown lights and the grayer, sidestreet lights; we drove through small-town darkness; and we were safe until we stopped at the town's end, and I asked, "Would you? Would you take me again to the San? I'm not sure who I remember."

Straight ahead was unused country.

Turned around we could also pass my street again and the entrance to school, but we were already late, and Arthur said, "I don't want your Uncle Billy to worry."

Arthur was a slave, I thought, with a slave's point of view;

but he said finally, "All right then, I'll show you something."

All ways were dark, but this way deeply. We only knew what things were as we passed them, dark stands of trees, rows of mailboxes, wooden markers, the start of hills—up, over, over and down—down a narrow, brambled road, as in a story, abruptly turning and traveling upwards again to a gawky house with finials, deep porches, churchy windows. Here was a spinster closed for winter. I couldn't see inside although I tried.

"This was where your father came from," Arthur said, and I was amazed. My father, the mysteriously dead and only ever whispered about—Arthur knew where Father came from.

I said, "You've been here from the beginning."

On the occasions when Uncle Billy did the driving, we blurred past the countryside at speeds I wouldn't look at with the numbers grown larger, long and skinny, wavery as numbers were supposed to be in dreams.

Uncle Billy said, "I'm in a hurry. Just tell me, can you see the FOR SALE sign? Should we send Arthur to shovel?" Uncle Billy asked me, but he answered himself. He said, "Yes, that's what we'll do. We'll get Arthur onto it."

Arthur found my mother's missing glove in the shoveling. He used the sharp edge of the shovel on the ice to get it out, her glove—one of the last parts left of what had happened to Mother at her own house.

✝ ✝ ✝

Mother wrote back from her Florida, "So you remembered making a snow car! I'm sorry I didn't see it. Do you remember how we used to dance to the Spanish music?"

I remembered more than that. That was the winter Mother never left the house but waved at me from windows to come in. "Come in, please! Come in!" she called from the house, the one I put my mouth to. Lip-prints or breath against the mirrors and windows, in such ways I could taste myself and the loose-earth taste of the house. We conversed lovingly, the house and I. Everything was in its place and sensate and easily hurt. The front stairs often felt neglected, and the basement knew itself as ugly. Whatever was empty or kicked or slammed shut wept. I heard my father's closet mumbling.

I knew this house. I was there for the bird that flew in and scraped itself against the ceiling in its wild, bloody flight. "Get out! Get out! Get out, you fool!" Mother was crying, but the bird slammed against the wall and died.

I pointed out to Arthur where near the trees it had happened: Mother broke her nose and bled; but Arthur said what I saw was shadow. He said what I saw was leeched from fallen leaves, pinking snow. What I saw, he insisted, wasn't blood.

"Your mother," Arthur said, "was excited to go. She knew it was time to get better, and she urged me to drive fast." Arthur laughed at himself, saying, "She didn't really like to drive with me. Your mother said I was too slow, and I am. I have always minded the speed limits, but your mother likes to go faster."

✝ ✝ ✝

"I am just the opposite of her," I said, almost shouting it over Arthur's chipping at the ice with the shovel. So much noise for a long time—chalk-marks when he hit the sidewalk—my worried ears grew hot.

TUCSON

We never talked very much, Arthur and I, but I was in the habit of kissing him good-bye, and I was twelve. My mother had always encouraged me to be affectionate and kiss—kiss friends, boyfriends, courtesy aunts, so that in the car, alone together, I kissed Arthur good-bye despite his ugliness, and I believed, and Mother must have believed, too, that such gestures made others happy, and sometimes I got carried away and kissed Arthur many times. Everyone likes to be kissed was Mother's motto, and so I kissed him—eyebrow, forehead, nose—I kissed until Aunt Frances scolded I was too old to kiss the help like that.

But how old was I? Mother wrote she had lost track; sometimes I was two, other times I sounded forty.

"I am almost thirteen!" was what I said.

"Too old to wear braids," Aunt Frances said. "We should cut your hair," and she stood me in a tub and slopped a drape around my shoulders and cut me very short. She said, "If you hadn't moved!"

Uncle Billy said, "It's perfect for the desert," and it was. It was easy swimmer's hair I was wearing when I was swimming in Uncle Billy's pool. On any desert spring night I liked to swim in the bath-warm pool, steam fogging the air where the light from the kitchen showed through. I could see them in the window, Uncle Billy and his wife passing, turned away from me. They must have thought by now I was in bed, but I was too old for such a bedtime. I liked to swim at night with not so much on as what even Mother had sent me—that stupid bikini! But now not a strap, not a bit of bandanna, I was just a body root-white in water and moving in a madcap dance, scissoring to get away from whatever danger I imagined, from kidnap or murder—but quietly moving, quietly. I did ballet: I stood on my hands and held my legs together straight for as long as I could.

"Are you watching?" Everyone asked this question of everyone else in the family.

I was swimming in my Uncle Billy's pool at night while the people in charge were crossing overhead. In the daytime, sometimes watched, I heard them say to me, "That's enough, Alice"—Alice, my name, after Mother—"that's enough in the pool, Alice. It's time to get out."

"Why?" I said, "I don't need anyone to watch me."

Uncle Billy was about to leave. He was wearing his cowboy shirt with the pearl snap-buttons and khaki shorts and worn-out two-toned shoes—he was dressed to find the Dutchman's mine in the Superstition Mountains. The jeep he drove was sufficiently supplied to prospect.

Uncle Billy asked, "Remember what I said, Alice?" He asked, "Don't you want a treat when I come back? Can you be good?"

"But why do I?" I asked.

"Because you do," Aunt Frances said, and she was giving other orders, too; she was directing the help, the nameless unreliables hired for the desert vacation. She was licking S&H

stamps for gifts. She was washing the dust out of everyone's socks *herself!*—rubbing the socks with a stone and saying, "Watch how you can make yourself useful, Alice."

Aunt Frances spoke of money, of Uncle Billy's, Nonna's, and her own, but not my mother's; what was left of my mother's was knotted in trusts and Nonna was paying for me—didn't I know that? Aunt Frances said, and said often, "Didn't your mother teach you?" Simple economies and healthful ways. There were rules, manners. Made beds and sailing spoons. "Napkins first and last," she said, "and the napkin ring is yours," and so it was, handwrought and hammered, a gothic napkin ring with my mother's name, which was also mine, *Alice.*

Alice, Alice, Alice, Alice!

"People who have spent their share of the family money are impossible," Aunt Frances said, and I guessed she meant my mother.

Others had often said to Mother, "Where does it go, honey?" But Arthur defended her. "Your mother is generous," he said. "She gives things away," and then he told me again about the stereo, the Magnavox, that speakered coffin with pencil legs, the box with shifting sound. He told how, at the end, before she went away, Mother had given it to him, had said, "Arthur, I can see you want this. I can tell from the way you pet the lid, you want this thing."

Arthur said, "I didn't have any records or even a place to put it." Like me, I thought, he wanted to see the long-playing records drop; he wanted to fall asleep to music. He said, "I don't play music in the car because I don't want to forget what

I am doing. But the Magnavox is home-music at night. The Magnavox is different."

I told Arthur that if the Magnavox had been mine to give, I would have given it to him. I said, "I would have."

I would not have done the same for anyone else, certainly not the desert help Aunt Frances hired, the nameless unreliables who passed spring vacation talking to me, complaining. They said they saw me as a fellow-sufferer; they said they had seen me swimming at night. Was I as unhappy? they wanted to know; and they told me about the troubles they had had—and were having—they told me about the troubles with Aunt Frances especially. They asked, "How can you stand it?"

They said, "The socks, the heat, that bossy woman!" Afterward they stole from her whatever they could carry.

On such a night when I was swimming, I saw them both—those nameless unreliables, those live-ins, shouldering a lumpy bindle of embroidered cloth, saw them driving off with Aunt Frances's TV in Uncle Billy's jeep, heard them laughing. "We would take you," they called out to me, "but we can't wait."

Aunt Frances was tapping my head with a spoon to say, You're sailing, Alice.

But I insisted I hadn't seen those unhappy unreliables back out; I knew nothing about it, their plan.

"Oh, come on," Aunt Frances glared, "I'm not blind. I saw you talking to them. I can guess what was said."

Aunt Frances was cruel, I thought, very rich but cruel, and Uncle Billy only sometimes took me with him on his jaunts and was forgetful and abrupt—as when he would not share his water in the desert on the trek. "Let that be a lesson to you, sweetie," he had said, while Aunt Frances had said, "Don't be so dramatic, Alice!"—when what did she know about thirsty?

"The reason we are rich," Aunt Frances said, "is because I am frugal."

Uncle Billy disagreed. He said, "The reason we are rich is because we are rich."

I was poor and tangled.

"All the more reason to cut your hair very short," Aunt Frances was saying. "You can walk through a dust devil and come out looking combed."

It dried quickly, this hair, even in the cooler, nighttime air I walked through after swimming. I was almost always dry by the time I went to bed; and only a few strands, still wet and queerly bent against the pillow, would in the morning come out kinky. Nobody noticed. Aunt Frances was checking socks—was I wearing them?

"Why?"

Spring, spring, I was dreaming, dillydallying it was spring when Aunt Frances scolded, "We are back! This isn't the desert! Put your shoes on!" She said, "We are back, and it is not spring here, not yet—maybe never. There's still snow on the ground. Look and see."

Dirty trails of snow were what I saw outside and the lawn, a thinning head of grass, a combed scalp—very muddy. Defeat was everywhere: dark shrubs, leathery and broken, and straw-dry plants on the shelves of the rocks, in shock, on end. The rocks were dripping tears yet nothing caught the light. Even the Emerald Gem was dulled: The mudflaps were muddy; the fender bumped up dust. Arthur was sick. His curtains above the garage were drawn; Aunt Frances sent Arlette with soup and sour bread.

"Why can't I see him?" I wanted to know.

"Because you can't," was the reply.

Arthur was sick, recovering from something serious that they said was his heart.

His heart—I thought of how it beat behind its black hatch of threads, slow or fast, depending on the orders he was given.

"I have never been late," Arthur had once told me. "I have never broken the law."

Never broken a bone either or buried a wife. No children, no hobbies, but driving, driving well, knowing cars and roads and the town we lived in and agreeing every winter to plow the roads, deliver mail, play Santa at the firehouse for the firemen's children.

"I get tired easy," he had said to me—how many times? "I just want my feet up," and in his house above the garage, I had seen him prop his feet on the ottoman and itch off his socks. His feet again! His feet were misshapen and shoe-marked, and I wondered had he stood on them when his heart attack happened, or was he found in the car, the car pulled over, the turn signal blinking—*his heart, his heart.* To think I had once let him carry me across the field with that heart!

Was it the size of him, was it that he was fat? Did ugliness have to do with it? Was his poor heart like the rest of him and poor, doing poorly, yet yielding to it, the crack in the wall that could bring down the house? Now that he knew where his death might come from would he run to it as Father had done?

FATHER

Surely having asked as much of others, I must have asked this of my father, "Then can I go with you?" But my father, I was told, drove off alone, and he never came back, which is all the story I got, and no more from Arthur, who had said the field where my father was buried was farther north of where we lived.

My Aunt Frances said to me, "You were five years old when he died. You don't know the man buried there. Even your Uncle Billy didn't know him—and they were childhood friends!"

She said, "You can't remember very much."

But I remembered riding Father's shoulders and fearing he would throw me off to feed whatever growled on the other side of the fence. I remembered being sick in his top-down car, the same he died in, stalled, adrift, moving off in rising waters broken up in spring; or that was what they told me: The waters took him. Those waters, rushed from the river that ran under Main Street, waters dark and skinny and mean, had swept away my father. Frantic waters moving out beyond the houses, the river was aflood whenever I was at the railing looking over, as my father had once helped me to do, lifting me to see the swell in spring. There was probably no way to guess how unhappy a man could be in the company of a child—and she, his daughter. There was no way of knowing what a man might yield to.

FATHER

I know this: My father loved my mother—*a truth*—and she went on loving him in a sentimental manner, polishing their wedding gifts and proffering me ashtrays initialed JCM. "You might enjoy this . . . ," Mother was saying and saying and handing me initials—his—on his silver napkin ring, a tumbler, highball glasses. Etchings of ducks, grasses, northern lakes, scenes done by an old family friend. I knew my father well this way, and I knew he was a dreamer, a capricious man shamefully departed. Mother took her old name back, making me one of them—Uncle Billy, Aunt Frances, we had the same last name: *Fivey.* I was my mother all over again. *Alice Fivey.*

Waiting, waiting, waiting for an answer to *Can I?* "Can I see Arthur now that he's come home?"

Time went by in the window where I waited for an answer and saw Arthur's curtains move now that Arlette had gone to visit. Arlette, with unsalted soup and crackers, would she show him what the day was like now that the snow was melting? Could he hear the water rushing off the roof or the icicles in heavy falling, ice shards and scattered birds, a day of drastic reappraisals: Arthur is hot and he is cold; I cannot visit him and then I can, and later still, I cannot—he is only just recovering. He is sick.

"Besides, who said you could go outside in just those clothes?" Aunt Frances was roughing my feet with a towel, repeating, "Arthur will be tired for a long time," and so sounding herself very tired. He would drive again, yes, she said, but the heavy work was done. The plow, the truck, the drywall rocks he liked to haul and lift and balance, work to outlast a man, such work, as had satisfied, was behind him. Gone the snow-night crossing when he carried me; Arthur was sick and would never be entirely well again.

Aunt Frances said, "Be quiet. That's how you can help."

The music, the rushed-hush of cars passing, passing us on a dark road, cars speeding, making a noise as if to call out, "What's the matter—you drunk?"

In a county full of straightaways, Arthur was too slow for where he lived. The cars passed by loudly, wrong speed. Arthur was amazed. Good citizen that he was, he did not drive over the limit while the other cars were sudden in their turns, wagging over gravel lots to get there faster. It might have been to home the cars were turning or to Friday-night fish fry when the cars bumped up behind us. The lights, swagged across the street and blinking, affected me like noise. The windshield was a rainbow, and I worried. "Can you see?" I asked. Snow was falling and the wipers streaked the glass. "Are you all right?" The way Arthur, now recovered, wore his good clothes carefully, ready to be buried, prompted me to ask, "Do you want to pull over and rest?" And we did; we parked near the school, on a dead-end street, and we slept in the car, and no one—no one in the long time we slept—passed by. I would have heard them; my ears were very sharp then. I could hear Arthur breathing in the half sleep to be had in the car, the one we both woke tired from and hungry. "But can you eat this?" I asked, breaking off squares of chocolate. "Could you have a reaction?"

What was it about his heart, I wondered, when his hair was yet so black?

✢ ✢ ✢

"Is it time already?"

"Do you have to leave now?" I had asked this of my mother, of Uncle Billy, of Arthur. Maybe even of my father I had asked as much, if I had known him, as once I must have known him: Father: side-part, bow tie, a voice radio-soothing when I thought of him. Now I had a car and rising water, a picture of a man driving willfully and fast . . . which didn't sound to me like him at all. If it wasn't an accident, it could not have happened, which meant my father was alive and living somewhere.

"I have never been," I said to my Uncle Billy; and "I have never been," I answered that first time Uncle Billy asked if I would like to spend spring in the desert, "but I like to travel. I want to travel." I made that known to them all, to the only living grandmother, even to such a grandmother as she, to Nonna, stroked speechless, I said what was purely true: "I want to see all of the country."

I went to Tucson again. While Arthur was at home with his trembling heart, I was riding horses. I was riding Patches in a stony river bed; I was swimming in the pool with Uncle Billy's full attention.

"Aren't you glad you kept your hair short?" Aunt Frances asked. "Would you like to go to town? Would you like to go to the cactus garden?" Every day promised some addition, more Apache tears for the tumbler, more stones for the jewelry we were making. Aunt Frances said, "I hope you know, Alice, that we love you." Aunt Frances and Uncle Billy both said, "We love your mother, too. You believe that, don't you?"

I didn't. I was making rings with Apache tears. I was pulling clear glue like skin off my thumbs.

Poor thumbs, my mother's, so evidently picked-at, sore. Her lipstick smeared on fast. One shoe, one earring, one glove, one of a pair always missing, she had said so a million years ago when I leaned under her crooked roof of arm, and she cried. Later she got mad; she threw an ashtray at Uncle Billy and rushed to hit him, and when he held her off, she ran to the glass porch doors and kicked in a pane and hobbled through the house tracking blood; but Mother wasn't afraid of blood or of dying or that was how it had seemed to me when I saw her leaned up against the front-yard elm in just her negligee, and crying, "He left without me."

Mother was so dramatic!

Mother was an embarrassment, a threat, a woman in a sweater dress and white bubble wig who had barged into Uncle Billy's house with me, her daughter, a million years ago. I was along—was almost always along—on Mother's sudden decisions to turn the car around and pay a visit. "What's this I hear," Mother had said that time at Uncle Billy's when she was in the bubble wig. "What's this you're saying?" with no other greeting, "what's all this I-can't-take-care-of-my-daughter shit?" Then that time we were driving with Arthur in my Uncle Billy's car, Mother had said it was true, Uncle Billy was right, she couldn't take care of me—not without a man anyhow, and the men she was picking weren't men. She was tired. She was sick of the snow. "Just look!" she said, and she pointed to fields of it washed against fences. We were driving in the Emerald Gem, passing shores of snow; and Mother, next to me, had her sad face on when she said, "You'll like it in a warm place in the middle of winter." Mother staring out the window at that hurtful brightness, saying, "Uncle Billy tells me the San has a beach—ha, ha. Now don't you wish you were going there with me?" But I was going to live with Uncle Billy; and I was going to visit his springtime house, the one he had built in the Arizona desert. The desert in the spring was tonic, the early morning hours and the late, red afternoons. The rim of mountains just beyond his desert house turned all kinds of red, and I tried and tried to reach them. They were farther away than they looked, and the desert was hard to walk for its unevenness, its cactus. Jumping cholla threatened everywhere; but I walked it, walked heedlessly against the bleaching sun in the morning, or walked in the afternoon through the glaucous paloverde trees. I walked in the bed of a dry creek where the stones powdered beneath my feet, and I thought I was grinding bone. The clack, clack of loose stone. Heavy, heavy me!

On almost any day, I was on my way to the mountains grinding bone and singing my story. It was my hobo's bindle. I carried it to anyone, to win friends and get attention from the teachers.

"Oh, oh, oh, oh!" Mother, on our melodramatic visit, our only visit to see her, was crying to Aunt Frances, "Why do you . . . ," and her lashes were coming unglued, so that she pulled them off, and her eyes, I saw, poor, lashless eyes, looked palely small. Her perfume was too strong; she smelled sour. She sat on the couch, dragged off her yellowed bubble wig and shook her head in a dog's kind of shudder, said *don't,* said *you don't understand,* said *so much bad has happened.* Mother scraped at her nails with her nails, which were also glued on; she took herself apart in front of Aunt Frances and me; she spoke of Father and the past.

"Why do you think?" Aunt Frances began.

The word *custody* was used, and Mother, I learned, had lost it.

"Oh, please."

But Aunt Frances went on: "Who else was there?"

"You wrecked it," Mother shouted.

"And that Walter?" she asked.

"I tried," Mother said.

Mother was crying at Aunt Frances on that shameful visit, when I thought everyone, *everyone* must be looking at us. Mother, grown too fat for her dress, was crying and shouting at Aunt Frances, "Then where are all my beautiful, beautiful clothes?"

"I gave them to the school," Aunt Frances said and told

Mother how she had taken only the raggedy clothes, nothing very good.

In the serious plays, I had seen them—the good clothes, too—the falling-leaves coat in falling-leaf colors on a girl, just the ghost of my mother, pacing the stage, erratic and grand, saying, "We can afford it, surely!"

The cost of Mother's flowers, I remembered; how the tulips, got in winter, stood up starched and clean as collars. Candles, candles—Mother had them burning everywhere after my father died. I remembered the candles and the Turkey-red carpeting, the nailheads in the leather seats. Everything was wrong for the town we lived in—not a neighbor knew what it meant, trompe l'oeil, though my mother had said it. Us, in the grocery, and stacking bloody wraps of meat. "Give me a million bucks," Mother said, "I would know how to spend it."

Mother had spent a lot of money on clothes, although many of the most expensive came from someone else. Walter had bought her the painted blouse, vines up the bodice, the Rapunzel shirt, she called it—light silk, easily ruffled.

Mother, I remember, in the Rapunzel shirt. Late May and the breeze made the garden blowzy—this way, that way— enthusiastic, and I could see straight-ahead to the pleasure of July, to the cut-grass green days of dewy midsummer. My mother could see it, too, days of it, from where we were sitting on the stoop together, she ruffled up in the Rapunzel shirt and the breeze that was blowing along Main, Lawn, School, White—our streets in the leafy splatter of late May noon light. I was happy, and it seemed to me that Mother was happy, too, in a purely quiet way—no talking.

✝ ✝ ✝

Even when her company promised no pleasure, I went looking for my mother. She was, as often, looking for whichever
man was making up her life. My mother made up a tramp's
sack of the silver and shouldered it to carry to a lover as a gift.
I saw her leaving, and later, on the lawn, I stood where she
might have stood, and I called after her.

"Remember my shoes?" Mother asked me when she had
stopped crying and Aunt Frances had left the room on that
one and only visit to the San. "My shoes in the yard with the
leaves?"

I saw shoes, narrow and balletic and made in a material that
stained. Strapped ankles, stubbed toes—from dancing? I wondered. Such shoes as these the terrible Walter caught up in a
rake as easily as leaves and burned.

Nothing then, nothing held its shape but blew away.

THE BIG HOUSE

The transactions I witnessed at the other end of the lake from Uncle Billy's, I didn't tell Aunt Frances—or anyone—I kept them to myself. At the other end of the lake from Uncle Billy's was Nonna's big house, the one she was wheeled in, sent up and down in by the Otis with the spring gate—me in the Big House finally, my favorite house with the elevator I could drive! I was thirteen—at last!—and left to wander. Three floors, eleven bathrooms, and bedrooms, bedrooms, bedrooms; the sunroom was all window, shelved in marble, a color green as of weeds or of weedy, shallow water streaked darker in places with amphibious nesting. The sunroom overlooked the lake; plants grew all over the windows, greedy cut-leaf light-lovers. But it was not warm in the sunroom, the sunroom was like Uncle Billy's house and cold. Nonna's parrot Polly was singing in her cage. "I like ice cream, we all like" and Miss O'Boyle, miss nurse, was feeding the bird ice cream to make Nonna smile. Miss O'Boyle said, "Nonna looks happy," but I thought Nonna only smiled to feel how cool the ice cream was against her long, split lips, how sweet. Miss O'Boyle said, "Next time you see them, you tell your Aunt Frances and Uncle Billy your *nonna* is just fine."

I did. I said, "Nonna has never looked better," but I did not tell anyone about Nonna eating off the same spoon as the parrot and soundlessly laughing. I didn't want anyone in trouble if what I did with my grandmother was wrong, was in-grown like old Nonna herself, was overfull of intimacies of the sort I had known with Mother. "I'm in the tub," Mother saying, "come and talk to me"—this easy we had been, and I knew Nonna's body just as well. Mornings I saw the folds of skin that was her back when Miss O'Boyle hefted Nonna into a tub and washed her.

Miss O'Boyle told me, "You make it easy for Nonna when you are talking. Keep talking."

I talked about Walter, who had followed my father and exhausted us so! So that, yes, I was glad, yes, relieved to be away from Mother and living in the Big House with Nonna. "Mother gave a lot away," I told Nonna. The bulldog clock, the malachite eggs, the Christmas spoons and lusterware. Also clothes, clothes, clothes—some of them mine. These betrayals of my mother shamed me but not enough to keep quiet. I wanted to sleep on Nonna's ironed sheets and eat rare chops with mint jelly. I told Nonna, "I never want to live with Mother again."

Miss O'Boyle gave me Nonna's hand to hold, so that I might kneel at the tub and speak close, "Thank you, Nonna. I promise I won't lose it," I said, but I was really like my mother and careless.

Nonna's eyes blinked understanding, but mostly she looked straight ahead and grew light in our arms in the water and floated, a small, grandmotherly, sleeping-sored body. "See those bruises?" Miss O'Boyle said. "She needs to be turned, and at night, you could do it. You could help," Miss O'Boyle said. "Nonna'd like that," and Miss O'Boyle smiled stiffly at

Nonna. "You like Alice to take care of you, don't you," she shouted.

But I didn't take care, or at least not that I could remember did I help Nonna very much. I often slept in the other bed; the best I could do was be company, but Aunt Frances on the phone said, "You're a big girl, now, Alice. You could help the nurses with Nonna." I talked instead; I sat with Nonna in the sunroom and talked and talked. I twiddled the desk gifts, a crystal paperweight with the company's insignia, a letter-opener and a magnifying glass, printed envelopes and stationery, and all of it from the company's president, long dead but still alive, Nonna's husband. (Just look in the foyer at the cane collection, the paintings of naked women.) The bench was his in the walk-in closet, where Miss O'Boyle dressed Nonna, and I made as if to help, wondering, did Nonna feel the pinch of it, her husband dead, when so much else hurt? Her back brace, her brassiere. I did help sometimes; I heard the intake of breath when we hooked her.

Him, him: Was it her husband she was thinking about when we strapped her in?

I lifted Nonna's heavy foot to the footrest on the wheelchair and wrapped the heel loop, which sometimes cut, with toweling.

Again and again, Miss O'Boyle had found blood on clothes, yet Nonna would wear them, the day-suits that hurt. She got red in the face whenever Miss O'Boyle tucked a tasseled throw over her legs.

Head shaking *No!* against it, Nonna wanted to be dressed in the dresses she had always worn—in long, knit suits, faux-belted.

Please! twisted Nonna's face when Miss O'Boyle was ready-
ing Nonna for the morning. She wanted to be dressed for
breakfast! She wanted raspberries fresh, like I was having, not
mush. But Miss O'Boyle lifted Nonna's hand from the egg cup
and spoon-fed the patient boiled egg. "No one listens to me,"
was what I saw Nonna saying. Using what parts of her body
still moved—her eyes, her eyes especially, which were big and
swarmy even without her glasses—she used her eyes to speak;
she put out her trembling hands, saying *No!* to the bed jacket,
No! But Miss O'Boyle insisted. She insisted on the sun in the
late afternoon, and she wheeled Nonna in it to warm her bat-
tered legs.

The sun, I thought, shone through her, through Nonna's
hair, her nose, her hands. And in the glassy sweep of windows
were birds. And, too, the flurry of her open desk—no matter
not much used. Here was life! Correspondence cards, hatches
full of envelopes, a folded sheet of stamps. The pencils I found
were sharp, and there was lots of paper to draw on. Greasy
lead, heat, the nearby TV's noise, and Miss O'Boyle saying *Really!* to it, not sounding surprised. Nonna was snoring softly.
Soon the cook would bring us cookies, then dinner, then Polly
the parrot and Nonna were spoon-fed dessert.

I didn't tell anyone how I liked these afternoons, these
nights.

Something else I never told Aunt Frances or Uncle Billy, how
outside the Big House, down the hill of stone steps to the boathouse where the boats hung by chains under canvas drapery,
near to where the pier was piled up and also covered against
the snow, at the lookout of the prickly cedars, I saw, I saw a

car fall through the ice. I saw the ice crack and steeple. I saw the back of the car sink. "Help! help!" I was calling despite no one near enough to hear me. The ice was thunking open and taking the car down fast, talking: small sounds from the car, the ice sounding, *awe, awe.* I made my own noises moving backward, hand to my heart, heel in old snow. I was afraid to run.

In the spring there might have been talk of raising the car, but I never heard it. I lived in the bliss of mystery. I was allowed.

I heard small motors crossing the lake.

I heard treecutters that sounded like my idea of locusts.

Nonna was snoring soon after her bath while from the kitchen came the Mixmaster already mixing.

Light ticktocked through the house, and I followed. Room to room to room, I went through Nonna's house on any day when I was not in school, and I was often not in school. Headaches, headaches, sore throats—I had a lot of these. I was sick enough that I did not have to dress and was left alone to wander in my nightgown. "Undressed!" Aunt Frances would have scolded, but I never told her. I never told Aunt Frances how many days I was too tired, too sick for school, how many days I had stayed in bed drawing or reading next to Nonna at her feet.

"Can I?" I asked, already starting, "Can I?" my hand in the jar of salted pretzels scrolled like the tops of old desk keys.

Someone else's clothes I found in every closet of the Big House. Doll-sized gloves! I split one up the seam twisting in my hand. Worse, I didn't put back what I had found; I broke the spines of narrow shoes, insisting.

I tried to be quiet: room to room to room, wandering.

My clothes hung in a room far enough away and which Nonna could not visit. The wheelchair was too wide; she could not fit through the door to see how it looked, my room, made up for me, ruffled and canopied and lit up by lamps that threw pleated shadows. Roses red forever were embedded in the door knobs noiselessly turned. Opening and shutting the doors then, out of the bedroom and into the bathroom, I went in and out and in and out a good part of the night on those nights I slept alone. A lot of the time I took baths. The water I ran at almost any hour was slow to heat and smelled of rust and wet stones as I bent to it: rushing water—rusty, yellow, then steamy—hot and hotter. Ah, underwater, then my breathing was as large as the voice I heard telling my story—I liked it.

"Do you hear me?" I asked imaginary children or someone else I imagined asked me. I spoke in many voices from whichever house I set the action—at Mother's, Uncle Billy's, Arlette's, Nonna's . . . on and on—and me in the story as the one who is watched.

"Can she hear me?" That was how some visitors started conversations with Nonna, asking of the nurses, "How has she been?" Asking such questions in front of Nonna about her diet, her pills, her doctors, her pets—about me, asking the nurses about me! "Having a teenager around doesn't tire her?" when just to see us together, I thought, was proof we made good company. I knew what it was when Nonna pointed, and I brought it to her: her reticule, her tippet, her toque. I knew the old names to old things.

"Can I really?" I asked, and Nonna trembled shut the clasp to the twisted rope of garnet. I never told anyone of all that Nonna gave me although Uncle Billy noticed gifts I wore.

"Aren't those Nonna's pearls?" he asked.

Once, making a fist, Uncle Billy banged on Nonna's screen. Once? No, more than once, but one time in particular he lost his temper. I saw him banging at the screen and whatever was being done to Nonna behind it. "Miss O'Boyle," he said, "will you please get on with it? I need to talk to my mother," but he didn't wait or he couldn't wait to say it. "Goddamnit, Mother. Why did you give to Alice what you always promised to Frances?"

I wondered what, of all Nonna had given me, did he mean? What did he mean now, and how did he suffer? I hoped he suffered a lot, and in this way, too, was the Big House corrupting. I hoped they all suffered. I liked it when I heard Uncle Billy yelling, "Daddy wanted me to have that prayer rug."

Uncle Billy and his wants: the Italian urns and most of the paintings, too, that much I knew. He put his name on the backs of the paintings; he didn't care who got the silver although someone would soon. There was to be a getting of Nonna's house. The cook, the nurses, the cranky Arlette talked about Nonna's possessions.

Arlette said, "Who would want to polish such a tea set for life?" Her hands were gray despite their work's gleam. Strangers to me, friends of friends of Uncle Billy's, all visiting Nonna and brought along to see the Big House, asked me Who would inherit? They asked me, "Do you ever get lost in this house?" They said, "What it must be like to live here!"

Sometimes I took them around.

I took them to the walk-in freezer where the plucked ducks, in their Nonna-colored skins, were bagged and shelved along with sacks of cut-up vegetables from Nonna's garden. Here were freezer-burned raspberries never to be eaten and industrial tubs of ancient ice cream furred like the berries, fringed with freeze. "Only the parrot will eat this stuff" was the story I told the strangers, and then I took them to see the parrot as proof.

"This is the sunroom, but the marble keeps it cool," I said, "even in the summer."

"And the boathouse, yes, down all those steps."

"The library."

"His sailing trophies."

"The library again."

"He liked naked women."

"We could even have a fire. Arthur will lay it. He helps here, too; there are no other men. Grandfather dead, Uncle Billy too busy, so Arthur does—has always—will do. He oversees the Big House. He makes sure of all of this, yes; Arthur is, yes, a bit overworked, but at any time he'll make us a fire."

Five fireplaces in the house, and they all needed cleaning. Eleven acres of specimen trees, terraced gardens, clay tennis court—this was an estate, and someone had to see to it everything worked, and that someone was Arthur. My grandfather was dead and Uncle Billy had his own concerns—who else was there then to see to it that Nonna's house thumped on? His great store of keys on the keychain he carried was sharp, heavy, seeming dangerous machinery, some of which started other machinery that helped the Big House to run.

Arthur was the one most in motion, but to think of the monotonous driving he did, how he drove back and forth, from Uncle's to Nonna's several times every day, and for a time, and almost as often, Arthur drove to what was Mother's house and mine, down Lawn Street past School. Our house, pretty thing, it made me wonder how my father could have left it. Perhaps he only wanted warmer—Florida, maybe—perhaps he was that way headed when the accident happened and he drowned.

The car through the ice, the fire up the hill. "Fire!" I told the visitors to Nonna's house, "Even though we live on a lake!" I said, "and there is all this snow, and the summers are damp."

The visitors said they hoped to come back in the summer to see the gardens and to swim. And sometimes they did come back these visitors, friends of friends, breathless on the landings. They came for an hour and stayed the afternoon. They wanted to see the garden even in the rain; the water they swam in was cold.

I didn't go in; I watched. This was, after all, for a time, where I lived aged thirteen, fourteen, fifteen, on and on in the Big House with the mystery of Nonna and all of her money.

TUCSON

"But why, oh why didn't you tell me about it?"

"Why didn't you tell me?" Aunt Frances asked. She said, "You should tell me when the help is unhappy. Now we're missing silver, but those women can't get far in the jeep."

In all of the houses I lived in, silver went missing.

Some of the help stole cars.

"But next time, tell me," Aunt Frances said. "Tell me if you think your *nonna* is failing—forget the nurses. Use the phone. Your uncle Billy has the keys to the house, and when the time comes, he wants to lock it."

A year, another year, summers passed, yet they still made up a bed for me next to Nonna on the chance she could be comforted with company. Poor, forlorn Nonna! In a crib for old babies, railed and castered and made up with blankets no matter it was ninety damp degrees outside.

"Feel your grandmother's forehead," Miss O'Boyle said. "Feel how cold she is!"

But what I felt was soft and cared for, an unnaturally healthy grandma, clear spittle on her chin and wearing a bib, sometimes needing to be wiped. Her eyes were almost always open and wetly watching me at night.

Miss O'Boyle said, "She doesn't want to miss what's left."

Nonna's eyes showed interest when I told her Arlette stories. How Arlette ate catsup on white bread and gave me eggs for dinner and wouldn't sit with me but ate standing up looking out at the river. Arlette's house was by the river and was the color of the river, a house—really a shack—near a mud-brown gush ridden by kids in tires near collapse. These river-riders waved to the passing houses; they spun in greetings to the bankside: *hello, good-bye, hello, good-bye.* But most people didn't wave back; they went on hosing down the porch; they went on fishing or working underneath the hoods of beat-up cars or burning trash or adding to the compost eggshells and coffee grinds—especially coffee grinds. I was too young for coffee when Uncle Billy first had Arthur take me to Arlette's house. Mother was sick and needed quiet, "a little bit of Florida" was what Uncle Billy called it, that place where sad people went for cures. At Arlette's there were different rules and different smells, mostly coffee. Everyone on the river drank a lot of it. The next-door mother spilled it in her baby's bottle to flavor the milk as a kindness—besides, what other kindness could she show her baby when she was taking in laundry, taking in dogs, taking in other mothers' toddlers. She kept her own diapered on a staked leash in the yard where it walked the rope taut, fell and walked, wagging a nippled-bottle in its teeth, or else it slept. Under the blaring sky the baby slept—dirt for a pillow at the mother's house next door, one in a close row of three on the river. Horseflies following everywhere here and sounds that waked me, late-at-night plashes of thrown objects—bodies, large animals, bedroom furniture? I was ten when I consented to stay at Arlette's but not so young I could sleep through such clamor. The question was who was fighting? Whoever had such energy late at night. . . . I had thought only Mother, but Arlette, glowering the counter clean, said it was the neighbors in the lilac-colored house. "Those stupid people make noise like that." She said, "They fight all the time."

Noise abrupt as light, and just as startling for when it came, came late in calmed weather with not even enough heat to explain the rage in the way doors were closed. "All the time," Arlette said, "they are screaming and clunking and gunning their car." She said, "They used to hear me." No one but Arlette in Arlette's house now, not so much as a picture to prove a Walter existed, some man so big she could hear him clear his throat and spit from as far away as the road.

And why not a husband, except that Arlette was as pretty as a dog-chew—Mother had said. No fun! Done for the day, Arlette stood stunned in the drone of the TV set, forgetting I was even there, despite my croupy breathing. . . . I didn't want to go to bed ever, but at Arlette's every door gave way to where she was. Her back was to the kitchen table and the lineup of old appliances. Our dinner dishes were drying on a dishtowel; the armless chairs were seat-stacked on the table, and the speckled floor was washed. Every night Arlette did this: She did for her house what she had done every day for others. I watched, being quiet, so that I might have company.

Nonna's wide-awake company, wet eyes on me!

I was thoughtless.

I wasn't thinking of Nonna when I felt my way through the dead-of-night dark to say *I'm home, Nonna. I'll sleep here if you'd like.* Me dressed and smelling of where I had been—some bar, some party, some car with boys.

I grew harder at Nonna's; I grew older—fifteen.

"Where have you been?" from Miss O'Boyle to me come home—blurry, flushed, plucked. This was the beginning of boys, of my own Bobs and Ricks, and I was late coming home.

Miss O'Boyle said, "You're just like your mother."

"You don't even know her," I said, but then neither did I: only one visit to the San before she checked out with some Walter.

Miss O'Boyle said, "I know all about her."

I only knew Mother was somewhere warm with a man she had met while resting. His name I forget, but he had been resting, too, had been a patient, too, if that was the right word for what they had been at the San.

I called Miss O'Boyle a bitch, and in private, a *fucking* bitch, but what did I call those boys—young men, beaux?—waiting in long cars, most often not theirs, waiting or leaning toward the passenger's door, saying to me, "Don't let the cold get in," saying, "Hurry. We're already late."

Sometimes I let a boy wait. Sometimes I never went out but from a far-off window, undetected, watched this boy go about his waiting. I watched what I could see of him, one of those guys who yet never rang the bell for me but waited motionless in the warm car. Perhaps his horn sounded faintly, and the wind took up the noise.

"Yes, yes, yes, yes, yes," I called out to the first serious man, a creepy boy in business school, I begged, "Please, wait!"

"You bring the boy in the room with you. Did you ever think of that?" This from Miss O'Boyle, Miss O'Boyle on some nights, who was sleeping in the chair but sleeping lightly and on her feet at my approach, largely waiting, saying, "Slow down, turn on the light, I want to see you!"

"Why?"

"Your aunt Frances, that's why."

"Do you have anything you want to tell me?" Aunt Frances asked, and Uncle Billy, "Is there anything you have to say? Are you meeting your curfew? Do you even have a curfew? You should not go out on school nights and on the weekends in by eleven. Eleven, twelve. We have to be able to trust you if you want to stay at the Big House. Do you think we can? Can we trust you?" Aunt Frances had the Garden Club and seats on boards in the city, yet she felt obliged to ask, "Is there anything we should know?"

I did not tell—I would not ever tell of what was spoken, of what was understood in the dark of Nonna's room when, on her side, she was watching. She made an answering sound to the noise I was making. She hissed or spit or slapped the bed by which perhaps she meant, "Don't do that! It isn't nice." But usually Nonna held still and watched; I saw the wetness in her eyes when somehow she knew where my hand was.

Wind, breakage, often water, booming ice. "Do you hear it?" I asked Nonna.

I rushed to Nonna's bed and was bending to her mouth to see, was she breathing, when she opened her eyes and saw me, and I was ashamed, jolted, almost excited. What was there in it for me if she died? Drama! I answered. Experience!

"What did you expect would happen if you didn't come home at all?"

"You don't know?"

"You don't, really?"

"Am I to believe such a story?"

"You know who you remind me of, don't you?"

"Your *nonna* said one time she accidentally clobbered your momma with a oar when they was on the lake. She knocked Miss Alice out. She said she thought your momma was dead. And I'm not saying this is true now—okay? but your *nonna* said the accident might explain the way your momma is."

THE BIG HOUSE

An old story was that my mother and my uncle Billy were fighting on the second-floor landing when he pushed her down the stairs in an argument. Nonna was watching from the foot of the stairs as her children, who were then no longer children, fought for possession of *The Clockmaker,* an oil the size of a double bed, a clockmaker at his work in windowlight, all fumy, red-based colors. Think of brandy or whiskey, think of whatever was being drunk by Uncle Billy and my mother and that was the painting's preponderate color—the color of what made them drunkenly fight this way in front of Nonna. But Nonna liked to watch them fight was what my mother said, and I believed her.

I believed Mother when she said the argument with Uncle Billy was about a lot more than money. Of course it was! Nonna's heart was ridged, rough, dry. The answer was simple: She only had room for Uncle Billy.

I believed Mother when she told me about her father's mistress, met on a train, although how would Mother know where he had met her? Still I believed Mother when she said the mistress had walked by Daddy on the train. The mistress was an old-fashioned milk-drinker wearing spiked heels, and Daddy followed her.

Daddy's mistress had a heart that wasn't bitter.

✝ ✝ ✝

"Do you believe everything you are told, Alice?" Uncle Billy had asked me in the desert. "Do you?"

Yes, yes, yes, I did. I believed that before Nonna's tongue thickened, she took her husband out of any story she thought to tell. She talked about her father, instead, and favorite dogs and Uncle Billy's travels.

I believed that when she had talked about my mother, and she had not often talked about my mother, Nonna frenzied helpless gestures. Talk, talk that was what Nonna did before her stroke, and after her stroke, too. I believe we talked, Nonna and I, and that she told me about my father. *There was a flood—remember—*and Nonna made waves with her hands.

My father gone away, yes, yes, yes, I was nodding; yes and the storms across the lake in air: stalk, leaf, stillness.

"What else, Nonna, what else do you remember? What? Are you awake enough to talk? Do you think I am like my mother?"

"Quiet," Miss O'Boyle was saying, "your grandmother is asleep."

When how could anyone sleep through snows that piled to the third-floor windows, rains that fizzed through screens and puddled sills?

The house was called the Big House, the Big House on the hill. It came with a horse chestnut tree and elms and oaks and a spruce tree I didn't like, and in the middle of the circular drive something exotic, seeming shortened and level-headed when in blossom.

✝ ✝ ✝

Nonna went on living to be ninety-something; my father was dead at thirty-seven.

Later, when I was struggling with calculus, Arthur ignored how we crossed county lines. He was talking along the long stretches we drove after school while I, driving, could only listen. I was driving Nonna's unused car, and Arthur was sitting next to me, instructing. He kept his window open and put out his arm when the sun was on his side. He told me that the medicines he now took sometimes made him sleepy. Arthur talked and talked and talked a lot about himself in the way he had when his heart broke and he outfaced surgery and came home well.

"This thing with my heart," he said, "made me ask lots of questions I never asked before."

I thought he was changed, too. He was careful in the way he moved. For lunch he ate dryly cooked fish he only flicked at with his fork—eschewing even relish, saying, No. No and a sigh were his gestures, but I was glad—glad!—we were driving together again, and I was at the wheel.

"Want me to park?"

"No," he said, "drive on."

And I did. I drove on through the spattered light of fall, the warm, monied promise of it, the light's saying, Yes, it is possible: Purpose might find me and success might follow. My father could have been a poet; it is not absurd.

✦ ✦ ✦

"It is possible your mother might come home," Uncle Billy had told me a long time ago, and I had felt afraid of what might happen if she did, and then she didn't come home, yet I was still afraid, often lonely—surely thirsty.

No one was ever as happy or as sad as she was, my mother, who might have come home to claim me, but she didn't.

Mother had used overcooked bacon for a bookmark or a hair pin, stick of gum, sucker-stick, twig—whatever was at hand. Her books were paperbacks, she said, and it didn't matter how the water-swelled pages fanned, dried, stuck together. "Paperbacks," she always said, "a great invention." I read the way my mother did. I was impatient. I cut the uncut pages in Uncle Billy's fancy books (sets of Tarkington and Conrad) with my finger for a knife until, found out, Uncle Billy took away my ragged *Bleak House*.

At Uncle Billy's I learned to read behind the curtains and the guest room's dresser skirt, but I could wander anywhere at Nonna's and read.

Books, the orphan's consolation.

"'That head I see now . . . has it other furniture . . . within?'" I wanted my own Mr. Rochester and found him in the shape of Mr. Early. High school English, last two years:

> *By seventeen I had guessed*
> *That the "really great loneliness"*
> *Of James's governess*
> *Might account for the ghost*
> *On the other side of the lake.*

If the head was a room, I wanted mine cluttered, stuffed, Victorian style. I wanted Mr. Early's praise, but the rebuking length of Mr. Early's sentences, and the speed with which he delivered them, often left me dumb and angry, and the only assuagement was he spit. Pinball body, angry nose and bald spot, Mr. Early was a class joke except for what he said when he spoke; then the dwarfing capaciousness of his complex speech and the seriousness of his sentiments made us quiet.

Once, bending to where I sat shaking my hand out of cramp, he rolled my pen into the pencil groove, stroked my arm, and spoke: "Dear Alice, you don't have to tell the whole story."

Yet I wanted him to know how well I knew the story, better than anyone else because I was not like anyone else but special, inward, informed. I wanted to say: I have seen such things.

Days when, from nowhere, unappeasable, punishing sadness kept me at the Big House, and my name in the roll went unanswered, Mr. Early sometimes called to see how I was. *We could have used you, today, we needed you, are you feeling better?*

Yes! from Mr. Early. *Good point. Well put. Exactly.* I got this subject right. Mr. Early was excited, and I was responsible for his delight, and I kept him at his desk asking, *What do you think about* and *What do you think about . . .* and Mr. Early said, *You tell me.*

> "You bring back how the red-
> winged blackbird shrieked . . ."

Mr. Early gave me the poems by the poet with the goofy name, whose affection for his daughter made me sad.

Once I told Mr. Early that my father had wanted to be a poet, and Mr. Early said, "That's where you get it from. All the more reason you should," he said, by which he meant I had to do for my father what he could not now do for himself.

"I don't know," I said.

"Yes."

"I don't . . ."

"You do."

FATHER

The preposterous blossoms, candy pink and stupidly profuse, were in the night light strangely come as from another planet. But about time was what Aunt Frances said, "Spring? We never thought we would see it!"

Wash the windows then. Ruck the garden. Scatter seed. The dots of yellow in the wood, the spiked, green start of things: snowdrop and daffodil and crocus.

My father never came back—no matter what he may have promised. He took off one morning in the car we called the Mouse: gray, rounded fenders, a grill that looked like a snout and a decoration of chrome banding the hood for whiskers. The Mouse was a harmless name for a harmless looking car, and it killed him; or it was the water that took his life though he drove to it. The rolled-up windows imploded, sounding the glassy dazzle and rush of water as my father passed down and down in what might have been a lie, this story of how he died. I never did see him again. He was elsewhere buried after he was found.

Late spring, hard ground, then from out of nowhere nodding flowers and loaded branches.

FATHER

"Everything connected by 'and' and 'and,'" the poet writes on travel; I have some lines by heart. In the dark of the car, they occur; the words flare, and I see the driver's neck. Hairs curled over a collar, a creased skin—white or reddened—always damp is how the driver's neck looks to me. I will not touch him there—any more than I would touch my father there or the men I took for fathers. A father's breathing, I remember, a breathing close and wet in my ear. The beard merely scorches.

My father.

My father is a name and the black oily roots of hair in damp, creased places. My father is a cutout—stark, defined— a standard man as seen by me from behind.

I am seated behind the driver and considering his neck and rising water rising to his neck and the kind of cold it must be creeping upwards with the water.

The passing scenery is passing.

ARTHUR

All those years I was always ready when the time came to leave, yet Arthur teased. He said, "I thought you wanted to stay." Aunt Frances, too; my Aunt Frances said, "Now you're sure? We have room." Nonna was fretting when I left her, kneading the blanket's silk banding even as she turned to be fed.

I was glad to be the one leaving—for camps and schools and college—but my intention was always to come back.

THE BIG HOUSE

Old dead hands prayered, a draped arrangement of draping skin, a fleshy hem colored to look alive by the gentle mortician, Nonna was in the casket, and I was at her side, yet "the glazing eyes shunned my gaze," or that was what I was remembering about her as we drove to her interment.

Arthur had driven us—Uncle Billy, Aunt Frances, me—through a gardener's rain that gullied the tent as we stood at the site, Nonna's gravesite, brighter greens, June, plate-sized peonies beaten in the downpour, the coffin shiny.

Who can forget? some said. Description of the too long–alive, now dead. The homily for Nonna went on and on, and Arthur had to wait.

Who would have guessed there was so much left to say?

At the Big House everyone I saw chewed with his mouth open. At the Big House Nonna's lawyer sleeked through the room, nodding at stories, saying, "Yes, she was an amazing woman, yes, indeed."

Indeed, indeed sounded like my mother when she was being formal, but my mother was not here. Mother was in California, the state she called her home. "I can be a kook and not stand out," she often repeated when we spoke on the phone.

Uncle Billy had not spoken to Mother in a while, and he excused himself for keeping my mother uninformed, saying, "Your mother would be too upset."

By the time I told her, Mother said it was too late for her.

"I need weeks to get ready," Mother said, "and besides Nonna's been dead for years."

Aunt Frances said, "Your mother's not interested in other people anyway," which wasn't true, I thought; because Mother wanted to know about Aunt Frances, yes, and Uncle Billy. Mother wanted to know about them especially and asked me, she asked me often now that we spoke any day of the week and not just Sundays—Mother asked me, "How are your aunt and uncle spending their money these days?"

But how would I know? I didn't live here anymore; I recognized very few faces. Mrs. Greene's, Mrs. Greene's daughter, Arthur, of course, the Nordstruckers, Miss Pearl of Miss Pearl's (still alive!), the Miller sisters, Mr. and Mrs. Vanvogel. Uncle Billy and Aunt Frances moved among these and other friends they said were Nonna's but who were, in fact, theirs, as who was left alive that Nonna knew?

Death, a death mound, like those lumps in the earth Aunt Frances had pointed to as burial grounds for the Indians. Of course, Indians, Uncle Billy's found and collected arrowheads from the Potowatomis! Next to the case of sprung-winged bugs and other artifacts. Buckskinned men powwowing lake paths in soft-soled moccasins, they and their squaws and their sick-to-death children were turned into lumps in the earth where Aunt Frances had pointed. Nonna and Nonna's friends—even the absent O'Boyle—and Arlette and my father were turned into hillocks I drove past, touring the countryside because I couldn't stay at Uncle Billy's house watching the people eat with their mouths wide open—no. I didn't want to talk to Nonna's lawyer, so I took the second car and drove to where I could sit off the road and smoke.

I smoked and thought of Nonna and how she had outlived my dread of her dying.

I smoked and wondered at how green it was, June, green and cold, a bed of iced lettuce, and in the distance down the hill, the lapis-blue of lakes, one after another, as though the land were a lake and the lakes, blue stone, and skipped. How was it possible to be cheerful, and yet I was; I was oddly gleeful and merrily giant-stepping into my life.

Nonna left me money—thank you, Nonna!—and a large diamond ring and a double strand of pearls. I bought an apartment in a brownstone with most of what she gave me. West Seventy-Six, in the city where sunlight is expensive.

How did I know except that I knew and had always known what Nonna would say. How Alice came early and fast—rudely. The way she was. July 10, 1928, a scorcher. "Tubs of dry ice ringed my bed, and the smoke was impossible to see through. I could feel people around me, but I couldn't see them. Midwife and helper, and someone at my ear, fanning, but no one else. Although I didn't really look, I didn't open my eyes, I didn't want to see who was in attendance. Feeling was enough. I hadn't wanted another child; and if I had to, not a daughter. I don't like women, and they were all around me when Alice was born, ahead of time, loudly. The way she was. Forward and boisterous from the beginning. Even as a little girl, she had precocious ideas about beauty. Once Alice cut off the heads of my peonies and floated the blossoms in saucers. Saucers, and more saucers, everywhere. The house felt like a pond I was swimming through. Her father said then, and for years after, that Alice was simply artistic. Well, maybe she was, but the way she used the downstairs phone closet as a sketch pad was no amusement to me. Drawings of high-heeled feet, a bit of shoulder and neck, a woman's face on the baseboard corners isn't my idea of funny. I am from the old school. Stiff, phony—I heard her clichés, the repellent voice she used to say, *my mother*. But the stories she started about her father's affairs were the most hurtful. The redhead on the train, the woman Alice said was really her mother, and the story that she had been adopted and brought to the house and wasn't mine. Hah! She should have a taste of a midwife's stitchery! The coarse repair of what that girl tore. Alice is a cruel and hurrying person; the miseries that befell her she brought on herself. She was only eighteen when she met your father. He was years older with a college degree and experience of war. His father was dead. He was a sad sack even then. How old was he— thirty? But your mother insisted. 'What's your rush?' we asked. Alice! She should have known better than to drive with a man who couldn't drive; but even after the second accident, after he had broken her face in a dozen places, she let him take the wheel. It was his fault she lost her good looks. We all said, leave him. Poor boy. Moping around the house on a weekend without even the energy to dress. And what was there to be sad about? The man didn't have to work, mind you. He could go on sputtering poetry. Alice had money. Her father had made sure of that, but Alice should have married someone like her daddy. Her problem was she wanted. Alice wanted, wanted, wanted, on and on. She was expensive. She was spoiled. Her father had made sure of that. Alice thought if she filled a husband's closets with expensive suits he would wear them and make her a fortune. I told her she was a fool, but she wanted a family right away. She said not in a million years would I ever understand. Alice was mean—her father was mean—and she deserved what she got. I can't say I was sorry, but her husband was unhappy; he needed help; he shouldn't have been left home to drink.

"I am lucky Alice's father didn't drink. That's all I'll say.

"No, don't even bother to ask.

"All I'll say is Alice's father didn't spend my money and he left me with some. With a lot. He provided, but I was frugal. People used to money don't tend to spend it. I didn't, and yet my undergarments have always been silk, and most of what I wear comes from Paris. I like pretty clothes, so there's a reason Alice likes clothes although her choices are garish, fantastic, often in very bad taste. The drugs and the drinking have never helped. At least that's what I think. I don't know for sure. I have never much indulged. I like punch cocktails and after-dinner drinks, the kinds made with sugar and cream. Alice puts out that I like pills myself, but Alice doesn't know what she is saying. She exaggerates. She likes to tell stories. She tells coarse stories. She says what my husband liked about me were my breasts. She could write about the daisies but she chooses to write about shit. That's what I always say is why write about . . . when you could write about the daisies. Alice thinks I'm in bad health, but I am not. I am healthy. I live alone in a large house with a housekeeper and a caretaker, extra gardening help and cleaning and sometimes with my granddaughter—with you, dear heart.

"I have never had to worry about money. I did not fight with my husband. When I was angry at him, I bought myself some jewelry. No, I am not leaving your mother my diamond. I am leaving your mother snarled in trusts she will never un-knot. She expects to get my pearls, but she is in for a surprise, and maybe I'll just give the ring to you. I might just leave you the sparkler.

"Here's the key to where I keep it. Open that drawer and see."

FATHER

I found him, I think, my own. Late summer in a far-afield family site, I stood at his grave and tried to communicate. A radio played from somewhere loudly, and I couldn't think what I was to him or would have wanted to be with this racket going on. Tunes from the 1960s, for Christ's sake, and coy impatiens growing so easily around his stone, I couldn't think who he was to me—but some kind of father, surely.

MOTHER

Mother, or the woman who said she was my mother, settled in California, finally. That was where she finally went alone and where I found her. She bought a home, which she insisted was a first home because, unlike all of the others, she had picked it: a modern twist done in taupes and railings, built-ins, islands, skylights unexpected. More sun and more sun! On the days when she was well, she cut gardenias and floated them in silver ashtrays; she opened the terrace doors. The ocean brought a breeze; although she was halfway up the canyon, some few blocks from the beach, the sheer curtains caught the wind and looked like surf. I saw such days as these with her in the summers I went to visit—high-pressure high-colored days—Mother's cats flopped dog-wise on the driveway in the sun. "Don't drive over them!" this new and cautionary mother was calling from her bed.

I was driving now; Nonna was dead, and I was doing the leaving.

"But you only just got here! Don't leave. Who is there to watch TV with me? Can't you stay another week?" Mother said, "I don't understand how you can leave in this weather." She asked, "How can you?"

I told her it was hard, but it wasn't really hard to leave her, not at all. I had fingered the dust of split capsules and licked the insides of drawers. Waxes, razors, jellies, whatever I had found that could be used on the body, I had used it, powdering the mound between my legs and walking through the modern house fearlessly undressed and shaved. The air against the newly shaved part was a pinprick thrill.

I was interested in meeting new men, but Mother's friends were mostly women. The men who fixed her car, the gardener, these men she knew only in passing. California was women and cats and time spent on the flat, flesh-colored beach beneath the rusty cliffs near La Jolla.

Poor Mother in her mother's body. I thought about it and about my own body. I shaved obsessively. Summer to summer, my goal was to be hairless and smooth and all one color—tawny.

We often went to the beach.

We went to Sea World a million times.

"Vons," Mother said. "We need something for dinner." I criticized her for the way she lived.

Mother said, "I'm sorry I don't know any men for you," and she offered me her sticky wand, swearing, "It works, believe me. Try."

"No."

I knew the sound the wand made. I had heard my mother's voice swoop, and the consequences! Animals snarled in their clothesline-tethers or retching what was spiked for them to feed on, I had heard the calamitous tread of pets; I had heard the sounds of women singing off-key. Fires in the fireplace crackling in August, stalled cars, spills, glass, glass stepped on, accidents, emergencies, the wail once of an ambulance—for Mother? I think it was for Mother, but all of this happened when I was half asleep. Maybe I was dreaming; I didn't ask about it.

I said, "We're doing all right without men."

She said, "But we could use more money!"

We were laughing then, Mother and I; we were loud with what bodily pleasure there was to be had in it, in making noise, in breaking one object over another, in saying, *fuck, fuck, fuck,* why did we let them do it?

"But with Nonna," I started to speak.

"With Nonna you could have whatever you wanted."

"A respectable life," I said.

"Arlette there to make your bed for you. For money and the comforts money buys you lived with your grandmother, and now look at what we missed."

There were times I would have missed. The night she threw herself over the hood of his car—who was it?—to keep him from leaving. I reminded her. I knew enough to make her cry.

And she knew enough to make me cry, but she didn't, and she never mentioned Walter, my own, unmet. She never reminded me of all he broke. She could guess at what I remembered; Mother had had a terrible Walter, too.

"I really don't like to fly" was what Mother said as if I had asked, "Will you visit?" She said, "It didn't have to be this way." She said, "My mother. My mother, my mother, my mother was behind it," and then she cried, and I was satisfied but embarrassed and went to get us new drinks. No one visited; my mother mostly slept. "What time is it?" she asked every time she waked.

Nearly one in the afternoon, nearly two.

"I was thinking," she would start.

"What?" I asked. "Thinking what?"

"Of, of, of."

Oh, I was tired of finishing Mother's sentences.

It was time to go home now.

But I came back another summer to California and stayed until the books I had brought and intended to read stuck to what they were pressed to, and the stationery curled, and the stamps dampened, and the addresses in my book looked to have been written long ago by a much more serious, constricted person. The person I was here in California was always touching herself with dreamy half purpose, touching herself absently in front of other people—once, the man come to wash the carpet, in sight of him, I fretted and held my hand over, and I walked too soon on the carpet and left behind prints.

And shoes? I rarely wore them in the California summers at my mother's house, one of a complex, where she lived, a condominium complex beehived in the canyon. Neighbors only glimpsed; the condo staff sucking up leaves or vacuuming the pools, otherwise a terrifying quiet here. Only visiting children and small nippy dogs walked on glittery leashes by women who did not speak English.

"Hola!" Mother called to Bertita and gestured. She pointed to the sheets, the cabinets, the paper products. *"Mas?"* Mother asked, her nails ticking shelves nearly empty except for cat food. At least the house was well supplied with cat food.

But lonely women and shedding cats turned joke-depressing, and it was time to go home.

"Already?" Mother asked.

"Sadly, yes," I said, excited.

✢ ✢ ✢

Home then to the city I went and not to the site of our losses, not to where my father and Nonna were buried, but to a brownstone block, landmarked and ginkgoed, old trees—very pretty. Old trees, old city. New York, New York. Teaching was what I did for money. "I want to be a poet," was what I confided to no one.

"School starts in two weeks, Mother. I really have to go."

The woman in California who said she was my mother had how many cats? They were not run over; the coyotes in the canyon ate them, or that was what she said when I came back the next summer and found new kitties. Found new friends, too, while the friends from before were less friendly. Their greetings sounded more like a question. "Alice?" they said, as if, like me, they weren't sure of Mother's identity. From summer to summer this mother changed. Her shoulders narrowed, and the weight in her arms dropped. She was growing crooked and used to her bed. It was hard for her to walk. Her hips were replaced; and then, the next summer, the doctors were at her spine.

The doctors took out and put in.

She talked of bolts and special metals and her hip socket growing cold. She said, "When I drink, I don't feel it—the awful pain." She asked, "Do I clank?" She asked, "Am I okay?"

"Better," I said.

"Let me see," she said. "Did you ever hear of blend?"

My thumb on her lids, I tried to blend; but I could not

make her what she was, and what we both thought she had been a long time ago—beautiful, beautiful.

This woman, who said she was my mother, was not beautiful.

This woman said, "I give up," and then she drank. She liked grape drink and vodka mixed. She liked such food as made her retch and in this way was similar to the mother from before, the same who had said, "Think I care?" then used a razor on her wrist—too lightly but to bloody effect.

"Didn't they teach you this in college?" she asked, steadying herself against the bathroom sink, wiping at her mouth. "A friend of mine told me that in college anorexics rot the plumbing." She looked hard at me then. "All that acid," she said.

"I should go home now," I said.

"Why?" she asked. "We're just having fun," and she smoothed a part of the bed for me to lie on. She said, "Come here, I'll scratch your back."

The skin on my back was not yet loosening, and it was easy to be naked before her and lulled by her distracted scratching. We were watching TV, and the TV picture was growing larger, the set giving off heat. Even the show we watched, it seemed, was louder. But outside was quiet and closing in. The sky had clouded up; the sun surely had set, though we could not see the ocean. Soon it would be dark. Her touch grew repetitive and faint when the only light in the room was the fluttering light on TV.

"Shush, no talking."

"Was I talking?" she asked and fell back to sleep.

Like me, she had to sleep near a glass of water.

Also, I noticed, our feet were alike—cracked heels and

bunched toes. Nothing anyone would want to be in bed with, and a sign, I thought, those overlooked feet, that no one had kept company for a long time.

Mother fell into a sleep from which she yet kept speaking.

"What do you want?" I asked. She didn't answer clearly but played with her lips.

"I should go home now," I said.

At home, and witness to a clearer change of season, I saw my hair grow in—largely, darkly. Outside the foliage tendrilled, and the bees frenzied the playgrounds' sweet refuse—apple cores and squeezed cartons of juice. The market stands were full of polished gourds and knotted ears of garnet corn. The ginkgos yellowed; the backyard gardens browned—blow-weed and thistle, late summer's drift, and the swimsuits I had worn on the California beaches were packed away now, salt-dried. I was growing in. I was making lists and using the phone. I was letting people know I was home again and that the area rug, summer-stored and cleaned, could be delivered, the boxed blankets, newly banded, would soon be needed; I was home again and preparing for the record colds, for the short unlit days and suspending snows, for the frayed, iced wires, the shut-downs, the winds, the space heaters, the fires, the tireless coverage of the ravaging winter that is winter in the city.

The urge to loll in a warm place is the same wherever I go.

The palpable impermanence of the warm weather place we paid to get to—and never won in a raffle—Barbados, the Caribbean, all salt-white, wet, and chafing sand. It caught in the legs of my suit and burned. The terrible Walter, my own (more terrible than Mother's), bobbed, ridiculous as cork, in the foamy surf; he floated on his back as he might have sat at home. His white feet stuck out, and he wore his silly hat. Surly, threatening man, Walter was yet intent on being happy; but with his mouth open, he gagged on the water that washed over his head, and he draggled himself to shore. Blear, sore face, water rivering off his arms and legs—he was a disappointed traveler ready to go home.

"But we just got here," I said, and we were fighting at the floating bar, swimming awkwardly around, treading water.

He wanted a real drink—no fruit in it.

He wanted a steak. "Fuck this fufu shit," he said. "Everything here is skewered on a stick."

Then I was down the beach away from him and scoring dope.

He said, "You stupid bitch."

He said, "I hope you get sick."

Our bedroom was sealed, drawn against the flickering sea. Cold floor and filmy curtains, stony bed—I couldn't fall asleep here and smoked my way to somewhere else.

All the time the terrible Walter was counting his money. He was figuring the tips.

He was sipping whiskey in the sealed room after dinner, near the window, in the dark; and because the room was very cold, I left him alone and opened the bathroom windows to let in the warm, wet air. I took a hot shower, which calmed me—but not for long. The sealed room where we slept was very cold and dark, and Walter was in the corner, without his shorts on, drinking, and his body, I saw, was wildly hairy. He saw me looking at him, and he said, "I hate you, too."

All of the nights on that island, he sat in the bedroom and drank, and I sat in the bathroom and smoked, and we yelled out at each other horrible names. We cried.

I said someone else's name over and over, and he said someone else's name, too.

I said, "I want to go home," and he said, he did, too.

"But where the fuck is my home?" he asked. "Why the fuck did I move in with you?" he yelled, yet he would not leave the brownstone once we were home again and living through the city's spring arrived while we were gone.

A second spring passed before he died, the terrible Walter, still in the phonebook, at my address.

WEST SEVENTY-SIX

That dog! He used to eat his own poo, and you'd kiss him! Remembering an Arlette story made me rueful when in the next room Walter retched whatever was left besides what he had been drinking. Walter's lips were sausage-mottled, fat grubs I had long ago ceased to kiss, but why had I kissed him to start with?

I had been late, over an hour late, to where we met at a restaurant called Billy's—loud, close, dark, full of manly hands handling money. He ordered for us old-fashioned, expensive food which he paid for with an aggressive signature. I thought his illegible hand meant he was powerful. Also, importantly, he was older by almost twenty years. Hailing me a separate cab, he said, "I don't wait longer than ten minutes for anyone, but I did for you tonight. I will never wait for you again."

No man had reprimanded me in years, but this sweet-sour scolding I remembered—Mother's Walter, especially—and the charged feeling was the same, so I said yes when he called again, and I was not late.

The terrible Walter wanted children. Insisting on what we had and what we could have together, he said, "I'm not so old we couldn't try. We could have children."

"Why not?" I said. I wanted company, but by the time Walter moved into the brownstone not a week in some warm place or chops at Billy's Friday nights could make us happy. We argued and drank; we wept for being lonely; children were out of the question; children would never have helped.

The terrible Walter introduced me to a man named Carter who was married to a Mitten on the board of a best school. After the evening with Carter and Mitten, the terrible Walter asked me, "*Now* do you think you're important?"

Not since my mother had anyone hurt me with my own hurtful thoughts, and I felt sobered.

Walter was homely and heavy and old; he was coarse and lurid and prurient.

We did not like each other and yet perversely made plans for Barbados while he bossed me around and I lumped it being sullen. I liked and I didn't like being told what to do; I thought, Walter knew how the city worked, and then I thought, he didn't; but he knew about fucking hard, and he was crude and risky. He took me to unlikely corners where girls could be bought, but I didn't, I couldn't, would never although girls are my favorites. I thought, I deserve a Walter, and he must have thought he deserved me, or else why did we stay together, a year, another year until he died? Fucking was why. Fucking was respite from meanness.

Walter lay on my bed loudly servicing himself, saying afterward, "You owe me." He said, "Pay me. You've got some money. I'll gladly leave," so I signed to pay what he thought he was due on condition he leave, and then, of course, he died. On an ordinary day—Percodan and Scotch—Walter took up his worn, overstuffed folders and drove off in a taxi to the firm. His bridge-playing, genius friend, a man tilling millions, saw him take the stairs, but no one else he knew encountered him. They think Walter cabbed it downtown and up again without changing cars, but what happened after he came back to the brownstone? The depression on the far side of the bed was evidence he lay there on our sodden sheets listening to the radio. (The radio was still on when I came home.) There was evidence he drank, he took pills, he got sick. He phoned an ambulance.

Someone got the money he surely must have left.

Someone got the money I paid to his estate. . . . "Sign nothing with fine print," a daddy could have warned me, but I had signed Walter's document; I had said *yes,* I would pay him to move out, and then he did—forever. Only the document held up.

At least I was working. I was teaching at the same small school, a small job, yes, teaching, but work not without its pleasures—yesterday's student writing, "Why can't Jane see the good things the bad things have?" The steamy urgency of her hand, the felt-tip blots—I had to smile. The loud way she came to Mr. Rochester's defense, the caped, brooding Rochester, a man as ugly as my own Mr. Early, Rochester, who, in disguise, tested Jane and found her worthy; every year some girl fell in love; this year it was Anna. "I'd marry him!!!!!!!!" Anna wrote. "Who cares about his crazy wife?"

Mr. Early's wife was soft-spoken, estranged, and not crazy, merely sad was how Mr. Early had once described her. Now she was on the telephone, speaking quietly.

Mr. Early died in the droughted summer when I was twenty-seven, a number I remember because I remember the summer of that year when the exhausted, yellow trees browned in August and lost their leaves overnight, that was the year when bookstores (the close, piled, classroom kind and the silencing kind—often paneled—any kind really) really made me sick. Bookstore fear overtook me the year Mr. Early and Walter died. I was twenty-seven; I saw death behind every sentence: ". . . a faint mustache of perspiration appeared on her upper lip." Summer session classes. I was teaching one and so was Mr. Early. Miles and miles apart, we were teaching last classes when he died. Mr. Early died in a classroom—his heart gave out in a dashed, absurd coincidence: "I heard a fly buzz when I died. . . ." Mr. Early was reading this poem to his class when he collapsed at his desk and died a death so appropriate, a person might think he had staged it except that Mr. Early wanted to live. He had said so in letters; the last arrived only a week before he died. Long, typed, smally folded in a small envelope, his last letter came with poems he had written and signed. Odd signature he had. Half print and leaned backward, it was at odds, I thought, with his generous voice. He said a lot of his sentences started with the words, *How could I* . . . so that why should I be surprised by mine?

How could I have . . . followed by the banal list of things to be ashamed of.

I was young when I met Walter. I was still young though I forgot. And Mr. Early, he was not so very old when he died. Funny man, he had only grayed. That was at Nonna's funeral, last time I saw him. Mr. Early had said, "We should have coffee. We should talk." We stood looking at each other, standing in the slivery, leftover rain, nodding through condolences. Mr. Early said, "We should talk, Alice," and I said, "Yes, I'll call," and then, of course, I didn't.

How could I . . . ?

I drove around the countryside, saying good-bye to it all. Aunt Frances and Uncle Billy had retreated to the desert; they rarely called. I don't know why I didn't.

How could I . . . ?

"Okay," slowed-down, drawn-out, second syllable stressed *O-kays* from Mr. Early to stupid answers. I made a lot of them, but I was enthusiastic in my responses, excited by patterns and symbols and irony. I tried never to miss class though I had headaches that took me out of math.

One time Mr. Early looked in on me at the nurse's office, surely a father's gesture. "So, so Alice. . . ." Is this the most of his voice I can remember? I have to strain to hear him speak. "Let's talk poems!" Let's talk stories and novels. Why can't I remember more? He loved sound, the way a sentence sounded. Mr. Early did not hang his hat on plot.

His wife was a painter.

"This is Ellen Early," she said. Ellen Early, the loved wife with an unlovely voice, saying "I know how you felt about Ed." But did she, I wondered—did I?

He called me the worst speller. I don't remember what I said, but afterward I looked up every word I was unsure of. *Exaggerated*—I misspelled it how many times? I had to come up with ways of remembering. I wanted to be taken seriously although mostly I think I was cute.

Once out-of-doors, Mr. Early surprised me, and his expression, when I turned, was so suddenly and purely affectionate that whatever I had done to provoke it, I wanted to do it again. For Mr. Early loved me, yes, I saw this. Later he wrote me as much.

Mrs. Early, on the telephone, was saying, ". . . if it had to be anywhere . . ."

Were my letters to him as full of love?

His letters at the end had narrow margins; he had so much to say. I could hear his mouth juice-up as he talked. He was happy. He wasn't drinking anymore; he had given up his pipe; he had more breath. "I never really noticed dogs," in his postscript, "and now I see who they are, and I love them."

MOTHER

A lot of what I said was mean and full of blame and said to make my mother cry, but then, when she did cry, I was embarrassed (this happened often), and I went to the kitchen to get us new drinks.

She called out, "Come light up one of your funny cigarettes and blow it in my face."

After a while we were laughing. We were laughing out of all proportion to the joke of Uncle Billy as a young man in the desert, scuffed saddle shoes and khaki shorts and the kind of hat explorers wear in jungle movies. Uncle Billy! Wild Billy! Those skinny legs! Those prominent knees! We laughed.

We laughed, but Mother cried again when I told her Uncle Billy was no longer prospecting but swatting at shrubbery with his cane. I had seen him; I knew. Mother cried, and I felt sad, too.

How young Uncle Billy was when he acted as a father to me, this explorer in the photograph with so much boy left in his face. His stories! In one the prospector was packed on his donkey and sent headless into town. On the cardboard pinned to his pocket was the warning *Don't Come Back*. I believed Uncle Billy. I believed then that there was gold in the mountains, and the young man in the photograph, my Uncle Billy, would find it.

Uncle Billy was lucky this way. His pockets were always filled with big change. He bet and bought tickets; he took me to the horse races. I fainted in the stands and lost my money. Uncle Billy doubled his. "A lesson," he said. "A lesson there for you."

Good, of course, to have inherited money, but every man wants to make his own.

And Uncle Billy married money, too, which was another lesson, surely. Mother told me about it often enough. She recalled Aunt Frances's train, the size of her trousseau. "Linens!" Even Nonna was impressed. Inlaid furniture and monumental jewels. Mother cried to remember a tablesetting: Christofle silver, Baccarat crystal, Herend's Queen's Bird five-piece plate setting. "I know the names." Antique candlesticks, silver pheasants.

"Then why did she steal my clothes?" Mother wanted to know.

"You left them behind; she didn't think you would mind. She gave them to the high school drama club."

Mother said, "If I could only smoke one of your funny cigarettes, but I'm dying here as it is."

She said, "You could have lived with me after I left the San."

I reminded her of a visit to Aunt Frances's when Mother came in loudly, unannounced, and tore off the wig she was wearing and exposed her small head. Her own hair was scant, a scraped-back color, a slightness like the rest of those parts she covered up, painted on, glued over. (My father's fault! His terrible driving!) Mother was crying then, saying, "What's this crap I can't take care of my daughter?" In the end, I was glad she lost out to Uncle Billy and Aunt Frances; in the end, I was glad to live away from her. *I did not want to be different.* And I liked some parts of school. I liked Mr. Early.

"Oh," Mother said, "that pail full of worms."

"You never met him."

"Your *nonna* said."

"But Nonna wasn't talking!"

Nonna again. It often came back to Nonna. "If my mother were really dead," Mother said, "I would know it."

Mother, sitting on the toilet lid putting on sock-slippers, was talking about what she most often talked about, saying, "It's Nonna. I know the voice. She's telling me that I wasn't Daddy's favorite. She's telling me what I already know, but Nonna is still jealous of me no matter what she says."

Mother said, "It must have been hurtful to Billy that you got the pearls. And the diamond ring was supposed to be mine."

Mother, wobbling at the sink and flossing, spoke brokenly about Florida and what it would have meant if we had found a way to get there. "Your father and I would still be married!" Mother said. "If it weren't for them." *My family, my family,* the viscous slick of Mother's family gunking up the day, following her, asking, why can't your husband, why can't you? Mother said, "In my family—colds, flu, measles—that's all. No one ever got sick. *Unstable* was the word the family used to describe him. Poor Jack! They said to my mother: *you need, he can't, why don't you.*

Mother, using her teeth to open the aspirin, drinking water from the toothbrush glass, swallowing—close, fleshy, human— said, "I didn't want to be different either. I just was."

Mother said, "I was in the Garden Club for a while."

Mother, in bed, said, "Look at me! I'm under the covers before the birdies have said goodnight."

And so she was! But who cared? We were under the covers together in the warm dark when she talked to me about sunning herself in that aluminum coffin, the sunbed, called *Florida*. "I named it," Mother said. She was the one who used it to sleep in endless off-seasons. She was out-of-doors at noon, high sun—had to be—or she would never get any color. She sunned her face and stayed in snow clothes.

"Outside it was rimy," Mother said, "but I liked saying at parties 'I'm just back from Florida,' and their not knowing the tan was local."

Whatever became of Arthur's homemade Florida?

"There is so much about your own life you never know," Mother said, and she sighed, and she cleared her throat and shuffed the pillows, squirming into sleep-position. Then when she was comfortable and quiet in this way, I knew how to lie against her, close enough to be touched.

"Scratch?" I asked, holding out my arm, and I felt her fingers graze me, and then she fell asleep.

A car exploding woke her. "What is going on?" She spoke fearfully, "It's so noisy. What are you watching? Why are you watching that noise?" She said, "I'm hungry, Alice, aren't you?" but the food I found made her sick. Mother said, "Don't blame me, please." She said, "I can't help it. I have ulcers. I shouldn't drink."

✝ ✝ ✝

The next day we read our books in separate rooms. This was nice. The sad part was walking out of the dark and into the coarse kitchen light. Mother was at the table in her nightgown, petting herself—her hands, her arms. She said, "There's nothing to eat. What do you want to do?"

I wanted to wake up very early in the morning and get a head start. I wanted it to be next week and me in the city at home where I lived: *West Seventy-Sixth Street! New York, New York.*

IV

ARTHUR

Plot abandoned in favor of insight . . . I was reading old notes on the *Lyrical Ballads* when Aunt Frances called to say Arthur had died while driving a burned woman to the hospital. The greenhouse man, name of Niles, on Lawn: It was his wife. Aunt Frances said, "The fire happened this morning, a kitchen fire." The wife's hands were burned. All Aunt Frances knew was already hours ago: Arthur had died on the side of the road in the truck, had died doing what he had done for most of his life: driving a woman, hurt, to help. The burned wife said Arthur had pulled onto the shoulder when he felt it coming. He looked alarmed, yet it seemed he drove onto the shoulder carefully and put the car in park before he settled back and died.

Aunt Frances said, "Can't you imagine him? It happened on Highway 83 toward Nashotah."

I knew the highway. I could see the high, graveled shoulder of the road that ran along with the railroad tracks. I saw a strip of grass, some fringe of dusted green, railroad tracks again, and in the distance, cornfields, turned ground dried but planted. I saw myself explaining to the students what Wordsworth meant by "spots of time."

The new man, Duane, was waiting at the airport. He told me about the accident, and how the burned woman had watched Arthur die. Duane said, "It happened quick."

Arthur—thinking of others.

✝ ✝ ✝

Duane drove me on in silence past closer cornfields and lumbering barns and modest houses; we bypassed the town where I had lived with my mother, passed the road to Nonna's house on the way to Uncle Billy's with its garden of jutted stone menacing the path to the lake.

"Arthur would have wanted you here," Aunt Frances said at the door. "I'm glad you could come."

"Mother wasn't up to the trip."

"But your being here he would have wanted," Aunt Frances said. "He would be glad."

"I don't want to see him." This was later. We were having early supper by then, Uncle Billy, Aunt Frances, and I, and the cold-spring, brusque light made me squint; I spoke to my plate. I didn't like open-casket, and I didn't want to see Arthur's face rouged and his hair painted black.

"There will be a receiving line," Aunt Frances said, "but we'll be the only ones in it. You can stand at the head, you won't see."

"There was no family," Uncle Billy said. "We were the only ones. He left instructions."

Thinking of others, thinking of others—Arthur always.

That night I wanted to dream but I didn't; no promises or portents, no visions of the years to come, just pure, dark, dreamless sleep, then in the morning, Uncle Billy, at the breakfast table, talking family plots. His was on the north slope of the cemetery, where his father had gone, and he would go, too, and Aunt Frances was debating. But what about Arthur? Arthur was only one and obliged to sleep in a crowded row where nobody knew him.

"Why not with the family?" I asked, and then to Uncle Billy, "You're such an ass."

"Alice!" Aunt Frances said. "You're not the only one upset. Arthur was a part of our family. Your Uncle Billy and I have made all of the arrangements. And none of this ugly business is inexpensive."

Aunt Frances and her S&H stamps. Yes, I remembered her slimy economies, her slapping after dust.

"We've more or less taken care of Arthur these last few years, and we were glad to and lucky we were in a position to do it." North facing at the table, in less light, Aunt Frances sat to her breakfast, saying, "But what would you know, Alice; you don't live here."

For the funeral Aunt Frances wore a nubbly suit and on the jacket some jewel the size of a rodent. A rabid, clawed thing was crawling up her shoulder and the heavy folds of her neck to the harsh hair, dyed rust and shapelessly arranged—some nest!

When did my aunt grow homely?

When did she start to drive?

I followed her driving the second car, so that I wouldn't have to stay long at the funeral home but could go back to Uncle Billy's and read. That is if I could find my way back to Uncle Billy's. Aunt Frances was going too fast, was speeding through four-way stops and leaving me behind with more cars insinuating themselves, and I didn't know where we were going exactly, making a left and then a right in a neighboring town I had never known well and to a business I had never noticed. LEONARD CRADLE'S FUNERAL HOME was a sign I could not recall although it stood out like a marquee as we drove to it. She forced me to drive over the railroad tracks when the crossing gate was clanging down. She forced me to gun through yellow lights and to pass other cars when the double line said not to. *Leonard Cradle's Funeral Home, Leonard Cradle's Funeral Home, Leonard Cradle's Funeral Home* was blinking closer.

I shouted at her for real in the parking lot until Aunt Frances slapped me, and I slapped at her rodent.

"Is this how you show your respect?"

"Fuck off."

"Is it, Alice?"

"Is it?" from Uncle Billy, leaning on a cane, I noticed, from Nonna's collection—since when had he taken those? "This may be how people act where you live. . . ."

I followed them inside and saw faintly familiar town faces. Two women, one from the Piggly Wiggly where Arthur liked to shop and the other from Bold Motors, named Barbara.

Barbara said to me, "I know where you live," and she smiled a crooked, idiotic smile. "I can't imagine it," she said. "Will you ever come home again?"

"Home?" I asked back, and I hoped Aunt Frances heard me.

Who came through the line then? Duane and the unkempt men from Pat's Hardware, Mr. Philco, the bakery ladies, Rita from the dentist's, Victor's Drugstore, and others: They all said, *how sorry, how sudden, how sad.*

It must be sad for you to come home this way. When was the last time you saw him?

The last time?

I tried to remember while driving back to Uncle Billy's, but the back roads rolled up and down—a field, a copse, a field, a muddy trough with guernseys ankle-deep in muck, filthy—and nothing came back to me.

I wondered in what colored suit they had dressed Arthur, and why I thought it was turquoise when turquoise didn't make any sense except as a tuxedo to a prom. Was the coffin's interior turquoise? Should I have looked?

I put the car in the garage and looked instead at what Arthur had touched here where he had lived and worked. Here was an orderly garage glossed in a color called serviceman's gray that when beaded in water shined. *Fivey Farms,* hardly a farm, Uncle Billy's house. Labels taped on everything he owned in Arthur's unassuming hand—meek loops, short stems, no flourishes. His labels on the light switches dispirited me, their homely thoroughness, and I hesitated to switch on the overhead lights in the greenhouse where Aunt Frances coaxed into frail growth what Arthur then had planted in the garden. The garden just behind the greenhouse sloped toward the raspberry patch and what would be tomatoes and lettuce. Exotic, coddled, fragile fruits, like the fig trees, were covered in carpet; the strawberry beds were blanketed in straw, and only asparagus grew unimpeded by the fluctuating cold. Baskets, shears, twine for tying up—who would do this work now that Arthur was dead?

Aunt Frances at the funeral said, "We'll have to find someone, but I don't know how."

Arthur had said he wanted to see the country, but he had

only his Sundays off—and only one vacation in all the years. Totem poles were what he said he best remembered; but the soggy trip explained his understanding of Mother's need for sunshine: Florida in a box Arthur built for her to lie in. Arthur, on vacation in the north woods, slept fitfully. A week was all it was, and it must have been enough for him; besides, Arthur was needed on the lake. Uncle Billy needed Arthur to settle the groundswork, needed Arthur to negotiate with the quarry and so finish the rock garden; Uncle Billy needed Arthur to make note of the work to be done and to get estimates and to calculate the cost. *This is a big place, goddamnit,* Uncle Billy was saying. Electricians and tree surgeons, contractors, painters, sailmakers, plumbers—Arthur knew where to find such men, knew them by first name. Some of them, Ray, for instance, Mr. Hornburg and Gassmussen, were like Arthur and volunteered for charitable causes. Arthur liked to play Santa for sick kids, and Arthur must have had more of a life than this, more than just the one I saw in the garage, but I never asked him really.

Oh, all those many ways I didn't know Arthur!

He must have had a hobby—look at the way he kept the garage! He must have had interests—look . . . but I didn't, had never . . . hopelessly self-involved.

From the lake-facing rooms in Uncle Billy's house I saw the lawn's precipitous drop to a shoreline propped with rocks, and I went there and walked around the boathouse snarled with whips of forsythia not yet bloomed. Arthur *would* have to die in such a month as this when the light hurt, when the pinked bark of bare trees and sodden beds of last year's leaves, the simple barrenness of things, strained my eyes, and I could make out no shore but fuzzed horizon. Sad or thuggish month March, pricked with deceiving, infant colors: chick-yellow, baby-pink, and quickly fading violet. The forced hyacinth blooms, although fragrant, looked plastic; no wonder then that I saw cheap when I thought of Arthur's casket, saw turquoise when I put him in a suit.

I walked back to the garage and found the door to his apartment was open—so Aunt Frances had come, I thought. She had neatened his rooms. The mail was unopened and on the table, in her hand, was a list: *Goodwill, Gassmussen, sink.* I guessed she had been in Arthur's closet; Aunt Frances had picked out a suit and watered his exhausted plants: on a tiered and tottering stand, African violets, so dusty and rag-earred, they looked to be a hundred . . . almost as old as Arthur was, Arthur, here from the beginning.

I opened his bed.

The light turned the paper shades into tea-colored parchment, and the heat, not long off, meant the bedroom still had his smell, a close, fruity smell as of a used comb while the rough sheets on his bed were oddly odorless. I shuffed my feet under the covers, then curled and was still and when I woke, I was not so surprised to be in his bed as to remember that Arthur was dead. When I woke, it was dark; when I woke, the driveway lights goldly framed the shades, halfway soothing.

Mother guessed she must have been sitting on the shelly edge of the Pacific, tadpoling in the ocean when Nonna died.

And what had she been doing when my father died? Did she remember, or was it up to me to remake him? I wanted to ask did she know *on the instant* where she stood that he was dead? Was she struck in the side as by a sword, was she blinded? Surely she was overcome when she was told, and then when it appeared to be a suicide? What then?

Mother said, "Suicide is Uncle Billy's story—not mine."

My father was meant to be on business; a briefcase was found in his car. A briefcase—certainly his—was found open, stuck between the seats, its paper contents in the current, its clasp a flash. She didn't know how anything looked; she only imagined the car under water and Father's body, still belted, knocking against the steering wheel in easy, constant motion.

Count the dead, a pile-up in months! A mound, a death mound, the kind Aunt Frances had pointed out when I was a child, and Arthur was driving us to town. Arthur, always obliging and patient, how kind he was to me; he only ever wanted to help me with my math; Arthur only wanted me to try the word problems.

"But not now," I said to Arthur. "Don't ask me to do that now."

I wanted to drive past our house, the first house, mine and

my mother's and father's. I wanted to dream over it, and, like my mother, see ghosts.

"But we don't have the time," and so we came back from town with stapled bags of pills for Nonna. We came back with soggy packages, me calling out to Nonna as I took myself upstairs, "Guess what Mother sent this time!"

Bits of cloth and cowries.

In California, Mother asked me, "What did you do with what I used to send you? Did you wear it?"

In Mother's stories of those times when we were apart, she was on the beach; she was sad in these stories but brave. She was sick, yet she had checked herself out of that slumberous place where her eyes were always greasy. She had checked herself out of the San—her name—and had left with the fat man, the one she loved best. Two crazies! Mother was thousands of miles away from me—and in love, too, with her fat man—yet she sometimes had to work at being happy. On the holidays she pretended it was any day at all—nothing special—just another island day, a high-July color, unadulterated blues and reds. "I wanted snow!" Mother said, but she pretended she was in the middle of an ordinary, midsummer, gorgeous day, not Christmas. She pretended she didn't miss me; and besides, she was in love at the time. She was in love in a new way, loving the fat man's imperfections, the damp white excesses of him— wheezy body parts, bad teeth, bulgy eyes in fervid glaze when he saw her. Close to tears, crying often, the fat man was real, not something she had made up. She could love him, and she did!

But I had heard enough. "Tell me something else!"

✝ ✝ ✝

In California, Mother made up a new past I didn't always know about. Once, mucking avocados for a California dip, a woman asked, "Do you have any of your father's sculpture?"

"I sold it all," I said, thinking quickly.

The guest said, "You're sorry, I bet."

I was sorry he never had been a sculptor, never had been an occupation a person could give details to. My father had worn a suit and dressed for a place I never did see; he swung a briefcase that was ruined with him. As someone once said—maybe even my father—"A man sounds like money when he makes money." Did his pockets chink? Did he carry more than pencils in his briefcase?

"We could always use more money," Mother said.

To the terrible Walters, to all of the boyfriends, we had both of us said, "We could use it!"

"You can always find things to sell," Mother counseled.

"I have," I told her, but I didn't always confess what of hers I had sold. No, I didn't want to tell her what I owed the dead man Walter, and I tried not to use any names that might hurt her. The woman, the one who said she had always been my mother no matter how far away she had lived, was sicker every summer, it was clear—more and more time, she spent in bed. I began to confuse her with Nonna.

"Mother?" I asked, standing near to where she slept.

✝ ✝ ✝

Little governess, light as cinder in a black stuff dress, she is tenacious of life and wants vision and practical experience and wider company. In another century she would not marry but would write. Jane would write—not Mr. R. Mr. Rochester is only confessionally garrulous, but Jane, Jane Eyre is a talker of such succinct or impassioned, memorable speech as in, how to avoid the burning pit of hell? "I must keep in good health, and not die."

My mother was once a talker. She named us all—cars and children. Then one summer she began to stammer. Living indoors in California, sleeping through the afternoon, she woke making thick and broken utterance. She could start a sentence but found it hard to finish. The next summer—worse—she couldn't begin. She had to be prodded.

"Mother? Mother? What do you want?"

Then, when she was dumb in this way, I was cruel. I told it to her face: I gave her a fuller inventory than ever I had before of what of hers was gone. Why did I tell her except that I did. The handkerchief table, the silver tea service. And California— when I looked up from the packing list, I saw that California, too, was disappearing. The soiled carpet underfoot was dank, and only the cats got fed. We ate stale chips for dinner.

"Who's driving to Vons for salsa?" I asked, but we stayed at home and went out less and less.

I said, "I'm nearly almost always broke myself."

Mother asserted, "We're in for it now, believe me. . . ."

One summer we stayed whole days indoors and watched the light move frantically between the slats of the shuttered windows. I lay in bed and wondered what had happened to Mother's wand. Her bedside drawer—I had looked—was empty. I thought about buying gel for myself, but more and more, like Mother, I slept. I slept until she woke and called out, "Look. . . ."

Nothing, junk—but we watched it. I got in bed with Mother and watched in the dark. Later, staring at me—me going downstairs for water—she said, "Why don't you take better care?"

Another time she said, "I'm sorry you're lonely."

But something about her voice, the way she spoke, made me think she wasn't sorry at all, and I hated her, and I said, "I wish getting old didn't mean growing ugly."

We had this in common: The men we had loved, and even some of those we hadn't, all were dead.

"All this to have happened already, and you're so young!" she said to me. "Really."

In California, I closed off, avoided, walked past rooms, living mostly in the bedroom and talking about what I would do if only I had money. I would travel!

Mother said, "Oh . . . have one of your funny cigarettes."

Mother scratching my back felt good, too, then, and sometimes Mother would go on scratching until her hand made a jerked motion, and she began to snore—most times lightly.

I let the TV flicker. I killed the sound. I rolled something small to sleep by.

"What do you think," is Dr. O's answer.

I think if I could only stay awake and concentrate on a soothing hobby all would be well.

I was hoping for the discovery of a rich uncle from Madeira.

I was waiting for the will to be read.

The years clacked past: Father, Nonna, Arthur, Mr. Early, and Walter, of course—the terrible Walter! my own, too full of toxins, still terrible—dead. The Walter-years, those years . . . made me sleepy, and the lawyer's secretary brought me water because I could not stay awake.

His lawyer asked, "Is this your signature," and I had to say it was, which meant I owed—for damages, for something—I had signed in front of Walter.

His lawyer said, "You can pay back slowly."

"But the months go by so fast!"

The yellow fall was almost past, and I was thirty.

I thought of hurtful people. My head was on fire with thinking of them, and I had to remind myself, in the most de-liberate way, to think of the kind and forgiving. Mr. Early, Mr. Early, Mr. Early, a teacher in college who went by his initials RWD, another teacher, an absentminded—*but brilliant!*—woman not to be trusted, and yet I loved her, too. She came to Thursday classes in a pleated skirt, silk, bowtied blouse, pearls; more than once I saw her face was half made-up, one eye scant of mascara. She was off-kilter in such ways. She was a tipsy mischief-maker at the end of the table, a quickly spilled voice, a gossip—dangerous! I wanted her for a mother when she had her best friends already—all famous—yet she said, "If you ever need help . . ." Did she mean I could ask?

"Yes," says the lawyer and he hands me a pen.

I can pay—I will pay—if I've done the math right it will take me five years. Not so bad.

Stringent and *inviolate* are words the students should learn; and some lines I ask to be read aloud, or I read them, "'Believe in heaven. Hope to meet again there.' What does this say about Jane's character?" I ask. The students make exasperated faces. Most of them get mad at her or don't care what she does, if only she would get to it. Make a life in the brisk climes, honest and alone, or travel with your lover undercover in warm places, but in less than forty pages, please! "Yes, yes, yes," I agree, "and why resist the sea and the comfort of his villa?"

MOTHER

I was the chief—our *only*—subject after Mother was moved from assisted living, from elevators, meals, activities, pets to the Birdcage, her name. The last home before the last. The Birdcage, as she once called it, the Nursing Home. Home! The word was obscene when attached to the swabbed, two-story, flung-out building with its enormous, linoleum sunroom. There, mid-morning, the half dead were parked in their chairs, and I found Mother asleep.

The nurses said go ahead, go outside, the mall's down the road. "She's best in the late afternoon."

Awake, Mother made fists and swung stiffly and helplessly at the nurses, saying she could walk, saying Arthur would pick her up, she didn't belong here, this wasn't her watch.

"Could you sign this, Mother?" I asked and held out bank business I didn't understand. I thought of my own damages; I thought to myself—don't sign! But Mother did.

The handwriting was thin, unfinished: *Moth.* "Your real name, Mother!" I shouted. "Write that." But Mother was become the shivery moth of her signature, the bald, breastless mother of the stories she once loved, the ones that told of women wide-open in pursuit. Their shrouds wisped, and the women howled; they traveled with potions and spells.

"May you be so lucky!" Mother had said and said to me. "May you never suffer like this!"

Now she hardly spoke. She could have been Nonna.

I show Mother her brother's handwriting; I unfold the recipe he sent. The formula to Fivey's milk punch: 3 quarts of milk, 1 pint of rye or blended whiskey, 3 ounces of *dark* rum, 7 ounces of brandy, 12 teaspoons of sugar, 1/2 teaspoon of vanilla extract; stir rapidly while mixing to keep the milk from curdling.

When I ask, "Do you remember milk punch?" Mother cries.

Tickets to the desert—I had accepted them from Uncle Billy; only now there was no message from him, no letter from Madeira, no comfortable inheritance to live on—and Mother was dying in a nursing home, expensively and slowly. Mother was hardly moving—straws in all the glasses, Kleenex, pills— the body's litter, skinflakes large enough to be identified, flew in a dust when the nurse beat her pillows. How many times had I been to the Birdcage? I sat in a small chair near to her bed and said, "I think it's nice here, Mother, don't you?" and she made as if to speak and then she didn't.

Mother was clearly, definitely, finally dying; and I had helped her to it, asking all those summers, "Can I get you more to drink?"

Returned, at school, I write on the board:

"'I had not the qualities or talents to make my way very well in the world; I should have been continually at fault.'"

Identifications. Give the significance of. The instructions are always the same: "Look at the clock occasionally to see how much time you have left."

FATHER

His bookplated books show my father had affection for bully-ing poets—hairy, bearish, mad. The poet found naked on the road with arms outspread declaiming Milton and stopping cars, this poet's books, in hardcover and paperback, and his collected prose and a biography and books of criticism take up an entire shelf. But what did my father think about?

I once knew what my mother thought about; she thought about expensive things and ownership, uselessness, loss. She had talked about the dead and was not afraid of dying because she believed she would join them—her mother and father, and those great-greats unmet. Whenever Mother spoke of her dead—and she once spoke of them often—I saw drifts of sheer hankies brushing against each other and so talking. Mother then had no plans for her body.

"You pick a place, Alice, scatter me. That will be fine," she had said, "that will be sufficient."

But I was talking about my father. My father is buried far from the church he attended in the years that he was married. Six. The years seem not so many now. Six years married. Twenty-five years now dead. Dead at thirty-seven, of an acci-dent, a car accident (they said), drowning. A morning storm caught so many cars on their way to work, they said.

"Besides," they said, "he was a bad driver."

They said, "Read the papers from the time. His name is there."

A mean rain runneled over blinded cars stalled along the highway on the day my father died. Spring. He took the old road that ran along the lake and somehow—was it slick or fog?—slipped off the road and onto the lake where the rain-pocked ice gave way on a breath and down went the car and its driver. Minutes was all it took. Eight, nine, ten, my guess. Ten, my age, when age began to matter, and Mother's terrible Walter said, "You look good enough to eat," and he licked his lips at me and farted. But my father—

Sometimes it is not the lake but a river that feeds into the lake that drowns him. There is no briefcase in the river, no falling through peated water. When my father drowns in the river, he is naked. The water carries his body fast.

My father has no body. No spittled lips, no smells. Fished out of the lake or out of the river, my father is washed feature-less, sodden and dark. I have to fight the impulse to kick him. "You!" I frown—a girl, disgusted—"Why is it always you I am thinking of!"

(My head is on fire like this sometimes.)

THE DREAM

He says what they all say, "We tried. It didn't work."

He says, "I think I'm only good for the money."

I grip the briefcase between my legs so that when he pulls, as he is forced to pull, the handle hurts me, but I don't cry. I say, "Daddy, please," and I watch him turn away.

My head hurts, and I am running after in my nightgown on the lawn. I'll do myself damage.

"I will!" I insist, knowing as I do that the use of a knife on a calloused place doesn't hurt so much, and there is blood enough to scare. "Look!" I stand on one foot with a knife in my hand, shouting after him, "I'll do it!" But he pays me no attention; he starts the car. He says, "I've seen that trick before."

"You want more?" I ask and make to use the knife on my hand, even though he isn't looking at me. He is headed in the other direction away from where we live, Mother and I, both of us cut up and calling, "Don't leave!" We are very dramatic.

One time Mother was on the bed, arms out, legs spread as one fallen back on snow, an angel-maker distracted by the task— cracked lips, eyes closed.

"Mother," I asked, already dialing. "Come quick," I told Arthur. "We're in trouble."

✝ ✝ ✝

Arthur got down on his knees and let me ride his back.
He made her Florida.

It was cold where we lived; I was most often thirsty.

MOTHER

Sitting askew in her wheelchair, Mother spoke to me of me. She said, "That Alice! She never visits!" Her voice, when she said this, was full of malice and glee. She looked mad. She said her hair was heavy on her head. "I can see as well as anyone," Mother said. "I know who you think you are. . . ."

I acted surprised and delighted when really I was afraid.

So many dead—Father, Arthur, Nonna—soon, I thought, there will be no one to remember us.

I sometimes said Uncle Billy's name on purpose and watched Mother grow frantic until she scared me, and I ran from her room calling, "Nurse!"

I didn't know a single nurse by name. I did not often visit.

"Any luggage?" they asked at the Gingerbread Inn.

"How long have you been gone from here? How long have you been away?"

And what's it to you? I wanted to say. I am not despairing by the roadside. I have more than gloves to sell if I should run out of money. See these pearls around my neck? I kept them after all. But I could sell them if I had to. Who would ever know what Nonna had promised Mother, then given to me, was gone?

So much gone. Uncle Billy had sold his house and Nonna's house and moved to the desert.

"I can live anywhere easily—have done." My boast, but I believe it. I am resilient. "Small but wiry" was what Mother used to say, and I am. Arthur would be proud. And Mr. Early, too, writing to me at the end, "I just want you to keep on going pretty much the way you are."

I miss the touching ways of men.

I miss my mother the way I think I will when she is dead.

"We never thought you'd come!" they say, these bent, wish-boned people, my Uncle Billy, my Aunt Frances.

Their new man says, "Howdy-do from all of us." He tells me Uncle Billy has a new project, a new wall, the start of a third terrace. They have their voices, my Uncle Billy and my Aunt Frances. They can see, they can walk, they can reason—the problem is breath, breathing, oxygen. Air! Tucson helps. Already a rope-thick vine, a cactus with inch-long, lion-like prickers, jags up the new wall. The desiccated landscape with its menacing cactus is exquisitely, adamantly alive, though it looks dead.

"Look what he's done," Aunt Frances says: walls, awnings, raised beds, gardens. The lap pool's blue-black tiles color the water such a blue I want to dive in—immediately! And the water, I am sure, must be warm. I know the way they live. I know the room they will give me at the other end of the house will be far enough away for me to talk to myself. There I can blow smoke out of the skylights or crawl along the floor to smell the rosewatery smell of Aunt Frances. *"Mi casa es su casa"*—pliant pillows, tender beds, blocks of blue shadow to rest in, blocks of white sun.

A girl once, I used to grind against the paths, prospecting in the high-season. High-season: one of the reasons I am here, the other has to do with Mother.

I am the daughter, the namesake, over twenty-one. Do the nurses phone me first? Must I be the one to say no, to look at the accountings, to oversee the dribble? (Last month, her front tooth cracked off. At first I told the nurses no, we will leave Mother as she is, but later I said yes, take her to the dentist's. Whatever is the best he can do, he should do it.)

"I don't want this job much longer," I say, addressing Uncle Billy, but Aunt Frances speaks for them both.

"We're too old, Alice," she says. "Uncle Billy has trouble breathing."

In the house of complete collections was there ever any room for children?

Aunt Frances says, "We have our money, it is true. Lots of money. Nevertheless, I balance my checkbook, don't you?"

"I have decided on a long time between visits," I say, talking at dinner about Mother and how it is with her all day in a wheelchair. She worries over the way the nurses have dressed her. She pulls at her windbreaker when it bubbles in the wind, pulls and smoothes with her trembling, twisted-up hands. Leisure pants, thin tennis shoes—her footwear need not be substantial: She does not walk. She sits after breakfast in her chair in the sun. She lists in her chair, and her toes point downward. Her feet dangle and point downward with a little girl's insouciance, and she scratches her unshaven ankles with her feet. From a distance, she is a little girl, but close up she is scaly, uneven, coarse and brown. The brown has to do with her mouth—and not the vague discolorations on her cheeks—but her mouth. Tobacco-colored spit stains the corners of her mouth. I am describing Mother parked in the sun after break-fast, growing sleepy yet fully dressed and expectant of some-one else. "I know who you think you are, *who you think*," Mother says when I step from behind the nurse repeating, "It's me, Mother, Alice. Alice, remember? Your daughter?"

She says, "My daughter is pretty."

"My mother, too."

She says, "I know who you . . ." She is disappointed. I think she does not like what she sees—and why should she? She pushes her dessert away and rocks in her chair. She looks very old, but Mother is the youngest at her table. Mother is the youngest woman at a table of women, all many years older, two deranged, one spastic, and they eat breakfast, lunch, and dinner together. Every day at this table, and yet Mother can-not keep up with the oldest of them, who snipes at her when-ever she plays the baby. *I should have been an actress* was what Mother used to say. The fork shakes in her hand—too heavy. She lets it drop, and then the oldest shrills at the nurses, "Don't feed her. She's not a baby. She can feed herself."

"Can you, Alice?" the nurse asks Mother. (Only the nurses know everyone's name.) "Do you need a little help, Alice? You like dessert. You know you like dessert. But maybe it's your daughter's here. She's here, isn't she. And you're excited. You're too excited to eat, aren't you, Alice. Alice," the nurses say, "this is your daughter, Alice. This is Alice, isn't this?"

Mother says to me, "I know who you are . . . ," and I think she does not like what she sees. I think she thinks my face is a pail full of worms, and Mother knows. She knows about beauty. She knows about death, too, only now she seems afraid of it.

Uncle Billy says he doesn't want to hear anymore! He is waving his hands at me, saying, "That's my baby sister you're talking about."

Uncle Billy says, "Come on. Before dessert, I want to show you something. I want you to see a new project."

His canister of air clanks over the stone patio. "You must have noticed," he says, "a lot has changed."

"Yes."

"Over there, the cactus garden."

"Yes, yes." Something newly made or found around every corner. Uncle Billy has taken his ease and enjoyed his money, his money and his wife's money, the piles of it. The *ha-ha* bets with his also-rich friends—"A hundred dollars says I can." Often he won, but how much did it cost, I wonder, to haul a lake for whatever was lost from a dead man's car. "It's there," Uncle Billy had insisted, drawn on by the corsair's adventure of finding the jewel case with all of Mother's trinkets, but why would the jewel case be in father's car? Mystery! Searches and constructions and destructions with powerful machinery and smeary men for Uncle Billy to boss: This was his business. What days tracking pleasure! I went along on the smaller excursions, to the Winter Boat Show and Oktoberfest and once to Little Poland. There we stopped at the Legion Hall just to jumble through the jumble sale, to see what merrymaking people were after. Uncle Billy bought me a netted bag of marbles, all color of cat's eyes and crystals—emeralds, diamonds, sapphires, rubies. Another time at the Falls, at a yard sale, we were walking through a dead lady's house. Arthur found a tool kit and Uncle Billy bought it. He bought a box of two-inch nails—never opened, never used—and a bread knife he thought Arlette might like. Uncle Billy had a care for everyone. Arthur was given a household tool kit, and Aunt Frances, a thousand-piece puzzle. He gave himself the nails. "And scissors. Good scissors. You can never have too many of these, Alice. Pick a pair." When Uncle Billy looked at me in this way and talked directly and cheerfully about our life, I was happy, and I wanted to walk the yard sale again, but he changed direction. His sudden, wandering attention made him turn away in a loose, goofy, goose-stepping way that yet wasn't funny to me, that seemed cruel to me. How could he lose interest in what we were doing together, but he did and was speaking to himself. "I've got a plan," he was saying when I had caught up near the car, and we were off again, Arthur driving. Uncle Billy with his lurched way of showing he was happy, his sudden, "Let's take a trip!" Wild Billy, Uncle Billy was looking at me, asking then, "Are you enjoying yourself, Alice?" Uncle Billy was bouncing in his seat, fussing with the power window— up-down, up-down—until he got it right. Right enough or large enough, first on the lake to put in his boat, first to hang it from the boathouse ceiling. Wrapped in canvas, girdled, strung up with chains like a winch-lifted animal, the boat I once spied through the boathouse windows wasn't used very much, even in summer.

When did Uncle Billy sell the boat, I wonder, and what is in the boathouse now? Who lives in Uncle Billy's house, and how have they changed it?

That house. I never thought the last time I saw the house

would be the last. The felt-lined, felt-protected feel of the house, how softly every light switch went on. More than the collections themselves—the seashells, arrowheads, bullets from the desert—the underlit glass cases of Uncle Billy's collections, the very glass itself, sobered me. I walked past with my arms crossed to quell the urge to kiss it, the glass, to feel it warm against my lips and see my lips' wrinkly impress.

I think I will not talk anymore about Mother.

"You're to enjoy yourself, Alice," Aunt Frances says, straightening my place mat, saying, "Sit down for dessert and enjoy yourself."

I enjoy the light, the enticement of the sunset when the desert is a softness that in noon-light was revealed as hooked and dangerous.

"I am not going to see her anymore," I say—I blurt really.

Aunt Frances says, "No more now, Alice, please."

"I am no help. I upset the nurses. I sit on the edge of Mother's bed and trip its alarm."

I am about to say more when the lights dim and the swing doors to the kitchen swing open, and here comes the cook with dessert on a cart. "Surprise!" says Uncle Billy.

"Occasion?" Aunt Frances says, "Must there be an occasion? No occasion. We are happy you are here is all, Alice."

Do they love me? Are we home?

Aunt Frances leans in, and Uncle Billy says, "Look," and the cook puts a match to the dessert.

Clouds blow up in the late afternoons. I read. I nap.

I walk in the desert carefully. I know about snakes.

I take a late-night swim in the lap pool and astonish myself with the color of my skin. My hair is not long; it dries quickly. I don't need a towel for anything, and I am not afraid of being seen. I am far away from the master-expanse of the house, and the house is asleep, and Uncle Billy and Aunt Frances are asleep. They are all nearly all asleep—poor Mother.

How did you get here? is Mother's question of me whenever I visit, and I wonder, how did I? Mother thinks I swam. Mother thinks *she* will swim, or else Arthur will drive her to Florida.

Aunt Frances has the new man drive us to the mountains in the jeep. Uncle Billy stays at home wheezing breaths and watching old TV. The cowboys skid their horses to a stop; the popgun action is fast. Uncle Billy is slow; nothing left fast about him. Uncle Billy must attend to his breathing, and so we are leaving him home and driving into the mountains in the jeep. The jeep is common; it has no name, is no Emerald Gem, no Mouse. My mother's names, all; maybe Mother is the poet? Aunt Frances is no mother, never was a mother, doesn't know. Aunt Frances is looking westward when, "What do you say to our view?" she asks. This has happened before to me: Two women, disparate ages, look out and smile at what they see, but so much of what I see turns into what is missing. Now it is Mother in the Rapunzel shirt when I am in the desert with Aunt Frances and watching where we walk because of hedgehog cactus, brittlebush, cholla; we walk into the desert to a bouldered clearing high enough to see . . . what? The distances remind me of the city. Two hundred acres Aunt Frances owns. She is philosophic: She says it really isn't hers, but when she grinds her cane against the ground, I expect it to bleed.

"I was a snowbird," she says. "I never thought to be here, but here I am in the desert, and I am happy."

Back at the jeep is the new man waiting in his uninspired clothes. Duane, Dale, Dan, Don, the new man is a kind of Arthur or that's what it seems until he drives us north and speeds. Aunt Frances says to him, "Not so fast, please. We want to see." But the road invites it, his speeding. "Please," she says, and he does slow down, but the road teases him forward, and he drives fast again, and then he is not an Arthur but one of those nameless unreliables, and Aunt Frances is yelling at him, the same way she yelled at all those other unreliables who balked and complained and stole from her. One of them stole the old jeep. The jeep we ride in now is sturdier; the drive isn't a clatter, but the speed is a problem. Why? Who is this? Who is our driver and how did he come by the keys? Aunt Frances is crying! She could be embarrassed. We are driving in a sheer way. "I miss your Uncle Billy," she says, and Aunt Frances is crying, and I am surprised by her crying. How dependent she is—and in love? All these years I have believed what Mother said was true. I can hear Mother in her brute voice saying, men are treacherous, love is petty, everyone cheats.

When we get home, the driver says, "I got you home."

"So you did": from Aunt Frances. Her hair is confused; her clothes look misbuttoned and odd.

Uncle Billy and Aunt Frances sit across from each other in the glassed-in patio. Their bodies, plump commas, are slumped in easy chairs. The sunset, too, is mushy. Aunt Frances and Uncle Billy look at each other, bemused, happily exhausted.

"What a day!" Aunt Frances says, and Uncle Billy agrees, and I wonder, will Aunt Frances tell him what the new driver did? They talk in code about the house and the desert: *And the garden? Called Mellor. What did he say? The same. How much? One fifty. Only? Yes. When?* Their patter! Aunt Frances says nothing about the drive home through the desert; she smiles right past the subject, leans forward, and takes up Uncle Billy's hand. "I think Alice was surprised," she says, and then to me, "weren't you, Alice? You didn't expect to see so much land." I am sitting between them at their feet, level with the coffee table, near the tea and crackers. Aunt Frances is petting Uncle Billy's hand as she speaks, keeping him in the room and awake. With some surprise I see again how she loves him. "Want a cracker, Bill," she says. (This, too, has happened before only with Nonna and a parrot.) Aunt Frances pours the still-warm sun tea over glasses brimmed with ice. The ice cracks and pops and is the only sound in the glassed-in patio. If I had any paper I would draw it, this scene—their hands, the glasses—but I would want to get it right.

ANY HOUSE

"I can live anywhere easily—have done." Said often. What a shrugged tough I am, a spoiled pouter at seventeen and eighteen and so on—me, insisting, "I can live anywhere easily—have done." Some of the bluster sounds like Mother, but this much is true: I am no stranger to working on my knees. I show up on time; I earn money. I wish Arthur were here and Mr. Early, too: just to see me! Still a kid! I miss them all, all the fathers.

THE DREAM

He winks when he sees me; he rubs his bristled face against my hand. Next he is driving away. Implacable wind snakes the grasses, storming. Upset sky! I am standing under it, but he is not. How is it then he can rub his bristled face against my hand? Against my hand and the inside of my wrist, my arm.

My mother, alive in the waked world, is much farther away.

He is dancing on his toes, springing sprung rhythm, whoop-whooping over the sound the poet makes:

Pitched past pitch of grief,
More pangs will, schooled at forepangs, wilder wring.

I read some of the same poems Mr. Early once read to us. The death-parts pinch more, and I have cried. I do not think Mr. Early ever cried, although he stood on his desk when he wanted our attention. I saw him jump around the room when the answer he wanted was wrong, yet he went on urging, "Come on, come on." And when I got it right: "Buy this girl whatever she wants!"

Mr. Early said a teacher has license to be loopy, to shout out favorite lines and sing, "Because she knows in singing not to sing." Mr. Early liked his Robert Frost.

I see myself at fourteen, still in the draught of father-loss, ashamed to forget, yet forgetting.

Mr. Early said the poets are forgiving.

I wander in bookstores; the fear of doing something ugly and private in front of everyone no longer seizes me. I have to summon it up for a fright, and I forget to summon it up. I am happy, happier. The newness of books for the young I teach, the way they read them as if no one before had ever rightly read them or understood them, the press and the pressure of loving books, a book, a book of poems, a poem and the poet who wrote it, and then the sorrow to discover the poet is dead! "We can only meet in air," says the dead poet. We mourn them, my students and I; they live on in their verses. I am the go-between in this romance, stalled in the clogged hallway between classes, in the breakup between classes. Even before they speak to me, they are out of breath and urgent and surprised by an older face close up.

FLORIDA

Wheelchair friendly and consolatory! Our weight triggers open the doors, and the walk to the ocean slopes through cared-for grounds: pond plants, sheafed grasses, and fanned things that sway. The trees at the shore are full of shade. The benches look out: blue solace and space. "Can you see the boats, Mother?" In the distance, boats, breasted, near the mark, then cruelly yank about. We are missing only their sound as they break against the water. "How?" Mother starts, then lapses into wonder.

I will begin with her father and his ever-polished trophies in their glass case: *Yes, he was a sailor!* and her mother from a family with old jewels in the vault, yet Nonna liked to be mistaken for the help whenever she was found in her garden with Arthur and his men, all of them on their knees in mud. "Deadheading," she explained to strangers come looking for the Missus. . . . Yes, the president of the company's wife looks like help, but this is her garden where one day her daughter will be wed. Will be? She was! At the top of the hill, Mother—my own—on her brother's arm, started down the rock paths carpeted for the occasion all the way to where the garden leveled theatrically, spaciously, and twelve bridesmaids, and as many ushers, waited.

Frances is matron of honor and William, Junior—Billy to everyone—Billy is playing Mother's father and talking of the gold to be found in the desert. He teases Mother. He tells a story on his sister.

Bad, bad girl, that Alice. What did she see?

Look at the matron of honor and guess. Frances, with her difference, her torch of hair, a red of such deep hue and thickness it forever inspires regret, Frances blushes. *She will fade,* they say. Surely she will, but on the day Mother marries, the lilt of bridesmaids in high color is a very garden itself, and the man my mother marries says so. He is a poet. He is a poet, and she is poetical, and they marry in Nonna's white garden.

The underside of leaves, the slime and slugs—no, no snakes, not in any of the gardens.

One year Mother is married in her mother's white garden and the next, in a different garden—shaggy, overgrown, more gingham than the damask of the Big House garden—a namesake, another Alice, is christened. Aunt Frances and Uncle Billy are godparents. They have no children of their own; but this child often visits.

Why?

Mother is tired sometimes.

And my father? What of him?

He looks like Ralph Marvell from the Wharton novel. He is fair and pretty; his profession is ambiguous.

I don't know his part and my mother cannot help. The tangle of live-wires I think of as her brain cross and spark, misfire, smoke. This, and the salty, cold fumes rising off the sea, worries her face. She blinks and focuses intensely on the passing shapes. Her eye's expression is as cruel as a parrot's.

The spectacle of Mother in the Birdcage dying: I do and I do not want to see it.

When I show her pictures of men I have loved, she says, "What a face!" and she frowns.

"Oh, Mother!"

Mother is a hitch, a terror, or an intermittent hurt. She is a black slot, a swallower, nearly out of money.

But what of this?

The wind is an assault and the sound of water bewilders her, and I wonder: What does she think? Does she think?

"I have to go home now, Mother." *Good-byes,* those little deaths, rasp my throat, but I am not sure she has heard what I have said. I am not sure she understands what we are looking at: so much water and the line that is the other side. Mother is in the sun; she is in her Florida. Squinting in that tin box of refracted light, she has to frown to see, and what does it mean what she sees? The world is a comfort and then it is a discomfort. Mother is all thin hair and vacancy, tears and starts, a small clutch of bones, an old woman, grown innocent.

Who will forgive me if I do not come again?

"Alice," she speaks, and she looks at me, and it has been a long time since Mother has used my name, which is also her name, as a good-bye, and I think she knows, as once she knew, what will happen to us. "Alice," she repeats. It may be no other words will follow or it may be a downpour of speech.